Birthday Cake
and I Scream

Look for these SpineChillers™

SPINE CHILLERS™

Birthday Cake and I Scream

Fred E. Katz

THOMAS NELSON PUBLISHERS
Nashville • London • Vancouver

Published in Nashville, Tennessee, by Tommy Nelson™, a division of NelsonWord Publishing Group, Thomas Nelson, Inc., Publishers, and distributed in Canada by Word Communications, Ltd., Richmond, British Columbia. SpineChillers™ is a trademark of Thomas Nelson, Inc., Publishers.

Scripture quoted from the *International Children's Bible, New Century Version,* copyright.© 1983, 1986, 1988 by Word Publishing, Dallas, Texas 75039. Used by permission.

Editor: Lila Empson; Copyeditors: Nedra Lambert, Dimples Kellogg; Packaging: Sabra Smith.

ISBN 0–7852–7494–4

Printed in the United States of America.

1 2 3 4 5 6—01 00 99 98 97 96

In a few days I was going to be twelve years old. You would think that a guy's twelfth birthday would be special. I thought so, but the problem was that the "party places" weren't cooperating.

I had planned to take a few of my closest friends to a paintball place. When we called, they already had parties booked for this weekend.

After we found that out, my mom and I called all over town for a fun place to hold my party. I think I heard the same thing a million times. "Sorry, but we're booked that night."

I had completely run out of ideas and hated the thought of uninviting all my friends to my party. I thought that would be the worst thing in the world. At least that was what I thought until Mom gave me what she called "good news."

When I came in from school, I tossed my backpack on the floor by the stairs and headed to the kitchen. After a long day at school and soccer practice, I needed to refuel. Chocolate chip cookies and a big glass of milk were the fuel of my choice.

I was pouring a tall glass of cow juice when Mom walked into the kitchen from work. She hadn't even put down her briefcase before she excitedly told me, "Kiddo (she always called me 'Kiddo,' but you can call me Mac—MacKenzie Richard Griffin's the name), I have good news for the birthday boy."

"You decided to get me a four-wheeler for my birthday?" I jokingly asked.

"No, it's even better. I found a place for your birth-day party."

My face lit up and my feet felt like dancing. "Where?"

"Spookie the Clown's Halls of Pizza." She beamed as she said it.

My face went gray, and my dancing feet turned to heavy lead sloshing through Jell-O. "Mom, we can't go there!"

She had a puzzled look on her face and asked, "Why?"

"It's for little kids," I protested. "I'll be the laugh-ingstock of the school and the youth group."

"Don't worry. You and your friends will have the entire Halls of Pizza all to yourselves." Mom smiled. "And Spookie the Clown told me that they have an entire room filled with the latest video games. They even have your favorite, Guardians."

2

"Guardians? They've got Guardians! Hardly anyone has that one."

Mom had a point. If we had the place to ourselves, we wouldn't be bothered by little kids. But I wasn't convinced. "What about the important stuff like—"

"Like pizza? You'll have all the pizza that you can eat," Mom interrupted. "Speaking of eating, if any of us want to eat tonight, I better get something made." Mom grabbed her briefcase and headed to her bedroom to change.

I sat at the kitchen table thinking over my glass of milk and three chocolate chip cookies. I might be convinced that Spookie's place could be a lot of fun, but I wasn't sure that my friends would be.

I felt uneasy, so I decided to wait until lunchtime the next day to tell them. They were all planning to be at my party on Friday night, but would they change their minds about coming when I told them that it was going to be at a little kids' place?

My morning classes went fast. As much as I liked lunchtime, it wasn't going to be my favorite lunch of the year. I was lost in thought as to how I was going to tell them when I heard Frankie call out, "Hey, this way."

I snapped my head up and noticed that I had been walking right past our table. I gave her and my oldest, best friend, Barry, an embarrassed smile.

"Earth to MacKenzie, earth to MacKenzie," Barry said, imitating the scratchy sound of an old science fiction movie. "Please land at your earliest convenience."

I turned to sit down, and I nearly plopped my body down on another friend, Lisa. She had slipped into the seat as I was snapping out of my what-do-I-tell-my-friends trance. "Sorry, Lisa. I didn't see you come up behind me."

Lisa smiled back at me as I slipped into another chair next to her. I was with my three best friends and I dreaded what I had to say.

Barry Lennon had seen most of my twelve years with me. He lived in the house right behind ours and was in the same Bible class at church. Our parents had tried to grow a nice row of hedges back there on the property line, but Barry and I crushed them down with all our walking back and forth between houses. His mom finally put a gate in the backyard hedges.

Frankie and Lisa were cousins and went to church with us too. Lisa was often at Frankie's house only a few blocks from my house. Since both of them had the last name Grey, we had sat next to each other in our alphabetical elementary school rows ever since first grade. Frankie and Lisa were the neatest girls I knew.

The three of us were on the same ball teams and went to the same youth group. I guess a person could say that we were inseparable. I hated to tell them my news about Spookie's.

4

"I have some bad news," I told them as a warning. I definitely had their attention and was ready to drop the news about Spookie's onto the table.

I had just opened my mouth when Davis Wong scooted into the seat at the end of the table and asked, "So, when do I get my paintball gun, and who wants to get hit first?"

Davis was the most recent addition to our little group. He had just started at the school this year because his dad was the new vice principal. We first met him at the youth group in the summer. He was a pretty cool kid, but I was finding out that he had a crazy sense of humor.

I didn't know what to do. I suddenly got nervous and blurted out, "The paintball place is booked."

"What?" Frankie cried out.

"No paintball?" Davis's mouth drooped into a gigantic frown.

"I hope you're kidding," Barry stated.

"No, I'm afraid that I'm not kidding. We tried everywhere. It seems that this was a very popular weekend to be born on. All the places have parties going on Friday night," I reported sorrowfully.

"So, what are you going to do?" Frankie asked with genuine concern.

"We got Spookie the Clown's Halls of Pizza," I answered.

Frankie asked, "Isn't that the new place in that old building on Tremble Avenue?"

"Yes, that's it," I responded.

Lisa gasped and got a dead serious look on her face. Then she jumped out of her seat and said loudly, "No, not Spookie's. Anyplace but Spookie the Clown's Halls of Pizza."

"I figured that some of you may not want to go because it's a little kids' place," I told them. My body slumped lower and lower into the chair.

Lisa shot back, "No, that's not it at all. It has nothing to do with little kids. Spookie the Clown's Halls of Pizza is haunted!"

"Come on, Lisa, you don't really believe that old ghost story?" Frankie asked.

"I've heard that people have seen some pretty strange things in that old building," her cousin said defensively.

"What does the ghost do, jump out of pizzas at kids?" Davis joked.

"Don't joke, Davis. There *is* something unusual about that building. Nothing stays in business very long there," Barry said.

"Remember, last year the restaurant was called something else. And the year before that it was Uncle Andy's House of Sandwiches. When we were little kids, it was the Chunks of Cheese Pizza Parlor. I can't remember all the other names."

Davis had a puzzled look on his face. He asked, "Why do you think that so many places go out of business in that building?"

"It's plain and simple," Lisa stated sharply. "The

building is haunted by ghosts, and they scare away customers."

In all my planning for my birthday party I had not stopped to consider that Spookie's was located in the old Tremble Avenue building.

When my friends and I were little kids, the older kids used to tell us stories about the place. They scared us with their talk about ghosts. But that was years ago. *We* were the older kids now.

Surely Lisa and Barry didn't still believe those crazy stories. Besides, we'd given our lives to Christ. Believing in ghosts and Jesus at the same time just didn't fit.

"Do you think the ghosts are still there? Do you think they will make a special appearance at Mac's party?" Barry asked us.

The bell rang before anyone could respond to Barry's question. As I walked down the hallway to my next class, I remembered those ghost stories the older kids used to tell us. There were nights when I had to keep a night-light on in my room because I was so scared. Just thinking about the stories sent a shiver up my spine.

Get a grip on reality, Mac, I told myself. *You've given your life to the Lord, and you're too old to believe in ghosts anyway.*

After lunchtime, the rest of the school day seemed routine. In fact, it was boring. Even soccer practice was boring. We did the same drills over and over again.

8

I was glad to get out of there because I was supposed to meet Frankie and Lisa at the town library. We were working on a history report together. I chose them as study partners because they were the two smartest students in the class.

When I got to the library, they had already started on the report. "Sorry, the practice went long. How's the report coming?" I asked.

"Not too bad. We've found a lot on the Civil War. Our big problem is narrowing it down to one main topic," Lisa said.

"Maybe I can help," I offered.

"We were hoping you might contribute something to this team. Sit down and dig through these books," Frankie suggested.

Before I sat I said, "I saw a book on the Civil War last week that had some unusual stories in it. It's on the third floor. Let me grab that and I'll be back in a second."

The book was way back in the corner. I had seen it when I was looking for another book. I remembered that it had personal stories from people who had been involved in the war. Some quotes from them could make our report stand out.

People rarely went up to the third floor. I remembered that the book was on the shelf in the farthest corner.

I passed the other old books with their musty smell until I got back in the corner. The light was poor there. Most of it came from a single lamp on a study table at the other end of the row.

After all our talk about ghosts, I was feeling a little frightened. My fear made me move very slowly down the aisle.

Finding the book wasn't going to be as easy as I thought. I kept looking, but it wasn't where I remembered it was. I was kneeling, trying to focus on the book spines in the dim light.

Suddenly, the light was cut off. A large shadow was cast down the aisle. What caused it? I looked up, but the figure was gone.

It must have been nothing out of the ordinary. Just someone else looking down the aisle. I went back to my search.

Then the light cut out again. I looked up, and I saw a dark form move away again. It did not look like a person. It spread out, as if it had wings, across the aisle opening.

I found the book and reached for it.

The light was cut off again. I spun my head quickly and caught sight of the form. It was tall and wide. Two small arms stuck out each side. I could see nothing else. That area of the library was too dark.

Gripping my book, I stood up and backed against the wall. My shadowy uninvited guest moved down the row of bookshelves toward me. The shape shivered as it approached. The silhouetted ghoul's progress was slow, and my fear grew with each step it took.

I scanned the shelves. I wondered if I could climb them and get away. If I tossed books at the ghoul would it run?

The form took two more steps and stopped. I placed a foot on one of the shelves to prepare myself for an escape. The shelf bent and nearly fell off. That escape route was out of the question.

I grabbed the heaviest books I could find and waited. If the ghoul took another step, I was going to clobber it. I heard it taking heavy, deep breaths. I wondered if it could hear my heart beating like a conga drum.

In the next instant, the dark, shadowy figure leaped for me.

I screamed and tossed a thick, heavy book at the shape. I hit it right in the midsection. The ghoul dropped to the floor, and the library light broke into my corner. In the next second, I saw what was behind the attack.

"That was just a little birthday scare for you," Frankie said through her snorts of laughter. They had carried Lisa's black raincoat with long rulers through the arms. The coat looked spooky.

"Hey, that wasn't funny at all. A guy gets really tense back in a dark corner like that. If I would had hit you with the big book I threw, it might have hurt," I chastised them both.

Lisa reached down and picked up the heavy book. She looked at the cover, and her eyes grew wide. "Very appropriate, MacKenzie. Did you choose this book on purpose?"

"No, I just grabbed a fat one. What is it?" I asked.

Frankie took the book from Lisa. She turned the spine my way. The book was titled *Our Town's Ghosts and Ghouls*. It was subtitled *And Their Favorite Haunts*.

Frankie tossed it my way. "Are you sure you didn't choose that on purpose?"

"No. I just grabbed a thick one nearby. I couldn't even see the spines of the books. Remember, you cut off all my light," I replied.

"Then this whole thing is spooking me. Is there anything in there about the building on Tremble Avenue?" Lisa asked.

I opened the book to the contents page. I scanned the contents and stopped when I reached the thirteenth chapter. The title under the number read, "The Haunting on Tremble Avenue." I closed my eyes and opened them again. I was trying hard to disbelieve what I had just read. Maybe if I closed my eyes, the words would change.

My heart increased its beat again, and I felt all the moisture leaving my mouth. I managed to mumble, "You're not going to believe this." Lisa looked at me curiously and I handed her the book.

"Look under chapter thirteen." My voice was barely a squeak.

Lisa gasped.

"What is it?" Frankie asked, concern registering in her voice.

Lisa didn't answer. She flipped frantically through the pages of the book. When she stopped, she began to read.

"The legend surrounding the building at 1313 Tremble Avenue is traced back to the turn of the century. At that time Bertrand Bailey Cooley died mysteriously in the room he rented in the building's basement."

Lisa glanced up at me, then turned her eyes back to the book. She moistened her lips and continued reading.

"Rumor has it that Cooley stashed a fortune somewhere inside the building. The means by which Cooley gained such a fortune are uncertain, considering his employment."

Frankie and I were riveted. We stared at Lisa as she turned the page.

"Cooley worked in the building's first-floor restaurant during the winter season. The rest of the year he was employed as a clown in a traveling carnival."

Lisa abruptly stopped reading and looked wide-eyed at Frankie and me. "A clown!" Her intonation was shrill, though she kept her voice low in the library. "And now a clown is running the restaurant! Don't you think that's more than a coincidence?"

"You can't be serious," Frankie said. "The guy you're reading about died almost a hundred years ago. No. It's just a coincidence, Lisa. Keep reading."

I remained silent. I knew Frankie was right. A clown who died almost a hundred years ago couldn't be linked to a clown who was alive and running a business today. But still, the thought was unsettling.

14

"Six months after Cooley's death, another man, Oscar R. Newcombe, died mysteriously inside the Tremble Avenue building," Lisa continued. "Newcombe, the manager of the carnival for which Cooley had worked, was allegedly in search of Cooley's hidden fortune. Newcombe claimed Cooley had stolen the money from the carnival.

"No facts were ever substantiated in the incidents, and no fortune has ever been found. Yet legend has it that the ghosts of Cooley and Newcombe roam the building, frightening anyone who threatens to find the hidden fortune."

I gulped. The fears I had as a little kid hearing the older kids tell me ghost stories about the Tremble Avenue building came rushing back. Fortunately, Frankie was still the voice of reason.

"Eerie legend," she said. "But that's all it is. A legend. There's no such thing as ghosts."

"Don't be so sure," Lisa answered. "The next section of the chapter is subtitled 'Reports of Apparitions and Unexplainable Phenomena.'"

"Hey, we better get to work on our report," I said. I didn't want to hear any more about ghosts, but I didn't want to tell Frankie and Lisa that I was getting spooked.

"Why don't you take this home with you?" Lisa said, handing me the book. "You can read the rest of the chapter later."

I put the creepy book under my arm and grabbed

15

the one I had come for. We managed to get some work done, though I had trouble staying focused. I wanted to get home soon. The sun was already going down, and in my current state of mind I didn't want to walk home in the dark.

The girls were going to Frankie's house a few blocks away from my home. We walked the several blocks from the library together talking about school, ghosts, the youth group, ghosts, other friends, and ghosts again.

I was still concerned that my friends wouldn't come to my party because they thought that Spookie's was for little kids. I wanted to make sure about Frankie and Lisa.

"Are you two still coming to my party Friday night?" I looked down at the sidewalk. "I mean, even though we can't have it at the paintball place?"

"Of course we'll be there," Frankie said. "You're our friend, Mac."

I looked up at Frankie. She was smiling.

"It will be a private party," I said in an attempt to play up the positive side. "Mom rented the entire place for the night."

"Aren't you two scared of that building after what we read earlier?" Lisa questioned.

"I don't see how a pizza place for little kids could be haunted. Isn't there some kind of law against that?" Frankie questioned.

I joked, "It's in the *Ghosts and Ghouls Handbook*."

We rounded the street corner, and the two entered Frankie's house while I continued to my house.

We lived on a dead-end street that was very quiet. Mom and Dad liked that, but sometimes it was a little eerie because of the giant trees lining both sides of the road. They blocked the streetlights and cast long shadows on the sides of houses. Four of those trees were in our deep front yard. By the time a person got to the front porch, the streetlights had all but disappeared.

After I pushed through the gate in the front yard, I thought I saw something move around the side of the house. If we had a dog or a cat, I might have thought it was our pet. But all I have is a goldfish, and it doesn't usually go out at night for walks.

I kept walking toward the house. I was a little unnerved, but I figured my eyes were playing tricks on me.

When I was halfway up the walk, I heard a crash in the backyard. At least, it sounded like a crash. Mom or Dad could have been dropping the trash into the garbage can. It could have been something that simple and that logical.

I tried to tell myself that, but I knew it was not the sound of the garbage can and I knew it scared me. I started singing a Petra tune to bolster my courage.

My shaky legs reached the porch, and I caught myself breathing a sigh of relief. As I let out the air from my lungs, something touched me from behind.

It felt like long tentacle-type fingers brushing against my head and neck. I felt the panic rise up from my stomach and form a lump in my throat.

I twisted to my right and lunged to my left, but the long fingers tightened their grip. I tried turning around to see who or what it was, but I was unable to move my body that far. It looked like the end of the birthday boy if I could not get loose.

Leaping toward the front door, I hit it with a loud crash and slid down the door into a crumpled lump.

No time to rest. I needed to get into the house. I used the door to steady myself as I slid back up.

Straight ahead the limbs of a large branch of the tree beside the porch swayed in the gentle breeze. I had been attacked by a tree. I think it was after my carbon dioxide.

Still leaning against the door, I was laughing at my carbon dioxide joke when the door swung open. I wasn't able to keep my balance again. And again I fell to the floor in a now bruised and crumpled lump.

"Your mom and I wondered when you were going to get home," Dad said.

I stared up from the foyer floor and said, "Hi, Dad. I thought I'd drop in."

He chuckled and said, "Your mom thought she heard an animal at the front door. I came to check it out, and there was our animal at the front door."

Dad reached down and pulled me to my feet. I snatched up my backpack that had dropped from my shoulder and entered the house.

"How did practice go? Did you work on your passing today?" he asked me.

"Practice was okay," I informed him. Dad was interested in all my activities. I felt pretty blessed to have him for my dad, and I wished everybody could have such a neat father.

"Katherine, you'll never believe what I found on our front porch," he called through the house to Mom.

She popped my plate in the microwave and poured me a glass of milk as she talked. "I called Spookie the Clown's Halls of Pizza today. Everything is set for Friday night from 8:00 to 11:00 P.M. I called your soccer coach and Pastor Daniels. Between the two of them, everyone should get word about the location in time."

"Thanks, Mom," I said. The rest of the meal I sat quietly thinking about the ghosts. I finished eating and put my plate in the dishwasher.

I wanted to get to bed early. I had a meeting before school in the library for a new club. Several of us read scary stories and wanted to gather our books together so we could loan them to one another.

I got to the bottom of the stairs and picked up my backpack. The light in the upstairs hallway was off, and the stairs ascended into darkness. My mind instantly returned to the thought of the ghosts, and I actually hesitated on the bottom step.

I'm going to be twelve. I shouldn't be afraid of the dark at the top of the stairs. Right, Lord? I thought. What I thought and what I felt were two very different things. It was a silly fear.

I started to climb the steps. My mouth went dry, and I could barely swallow. My heart beat as if I had just run a mile. I didn't like the dark to begin with, but my mind was running away with wild pictures of the ghosts of the pizza place.

At the top of the stairs, I gripped the banister and pulled myself around in the direction of my room.

I kept thinking to myself how silly I was being. Nothing reached out of the dark hallway and grabbed me. Nothing ever did.

I reached over and turned on the little table lamp at the top of the stairs. It was like every other night in my life. I hustled down the hall to my room and pushed open the door.

I looked straight ahead at the window in my room.

I screamed and dropped my backpack. A face with two large eyes was staring back at me.

5

I stepped back and tripped over the backpack, landing hard on the hallway floor. I tried pushing myself along the floor with my feet, but I made slow progress.

"What happened, MacKenzie?" my dad asked with a concerned tone from the bottom of the stairs.

"My bag slipped from my hand, and I tripped over it." I told him only part of the story, or I would have ended up going into the part about the dark at the top of the stairs.

I pulled myself to my feet, reached in, and flipped on the light in my room. My eyes went immediately to the big window. Taped to it was a round yellow smiley face. Over it was a small banner that said HAPPY BIRTHDAY.

I laughed to myself. My room was decorated with streamers and mobiles that all said HAPPY TWELFTH BIRTHDAY. My mom was crazy sometimes. I'd have to give her a thank-you hug in the morning.

After another look around, I shook my head and snickered. I put my backpack on the desk and got my pajamas out of my bureau. My body was tired from the long soccer practice and studies at the library.

After washing up and brushing my teeth, I sank my body deep under the covers. The smiley-face scare had jarred me awake. I needed something to relax me.

Digging through the stack of books I had ready for the meeting the next morning, I found one that I had read years ago. I was ready to read it when I suddenly remembered the book that I threw at the raincoat ghost. It was in my backpack.

I dug it out of the bottom of the pack and laid the heavy volume on my bed. It wasn't exactly what I would call light reading. The book must have weighed two to three pounds.

For a moment, I had second thoughts about cracking open the book. Did I really want to know about the ghosts at Spookie's pizza place? I knew they weren't real. Did I really need to read what they did to people?

Just like the monkey from my favorite set of children's books, I was "very curious." I stretched out on top of the covers and leaned back on my pillow. I pulled the big book up and rested it on my body. I popped it open to chapter thirteen.

I hadn't even started to read before I recognized

the fear overcoming me. *Here we go again,* I thought. *Lord? Sorry I get spooked so easily.* I was going to be twelve in a few days. I shouldn't be afraid of some old story about a downtown building.

I began reading where Lisa had left off that afternoon: "In the last fifty years, the large red-brick building that sits in the middle of Tremble Avenue's business district has seen more than thirty tenants. Many of the tenants and customers testified to witnessing strange, unexplainable disturbances.

"In the 1940s, mysterious sightings of a gaunt gray figure occurred. At that time the building housed Dandy's Five and Dime Store.

"In one instance, a customer had selected her items from one of the basement bargain areas and walked to the register. Without looking up, she placed her purchases on the checkout counter. While she was digging out her money from deep inside her purse, the items moved off the counter, and the register rang.

"The customer pulled her money from her purse and looked up to smile at the clerk. When she did, nothing was there except for the long kitchen knife that she had selected. It was floating in midair. When she screamed, the knife dropped to the floor, and she heard a haunting, eerie laugh."

Big deal, I thought, trying to dismiss my fears. The woman probably needed to buy glasses instead of a kitchen knife. Besides, that had happened before even my dad was born, and that was a long time ago.

I debated with myself as to whether or not I should read the rest of the chapter. As I said, I'm "very curious," so I continued to read.

"Over the years the building has changed hands another twenty-nine times. At the writing of this book, a new pizza restaurant for kids is planning to open after extensive remodeling. The previous owner ran a bakery that specialized in hand-decorated birthday cakes.

"The birthday cake bakery moved out after the last instance of a haunting. One of the nighttime custodians had gone into the basement to retrieve some bags of flour needed for the next morning's work. The worker said that he was 'attacked from behind. I didn't know what it was. I thought maybe a burglar got in until these long, gray arms wrapped themselves around me. I struggled as hard as I could, and the two of us fell into the stacked bags of flour. Several of them broke, sending clouds of flour dust into the air. When it finally settled, I looked around for my attacker. All I saw was a thin, grayish white form slipping into the next room.'

"The night custodian said that he didn't follow the ghost but immediately ran upstairs and then outside, never to return to work on Tremble Avenue again."

I stopped reading for a moment and rubbed my eyes. They were sore, and my mouth was dry. I wanted a drink of water, but I was too afraid to climb out of bed and get it. I decided to stay in bed and try to relax. I breathed deeply and closed my eyes.

After a few minutes I picked up the book and began reading again.

"The most recent disturbing and unexplainable event at the Tremble Avenue building occurred on September 23." Then the book gave this year's date.

Surely I misread that. I looked back at the page and read the sentence again.

"The most recent disturbing and unexplainable event at the Tremble Avenue building occurred on . . ." I hadn't misread it. It was this Friday's date. I felt my breath come in shorter gasps as I read on.

"MacKenzie Griffin, celebrating his twelfth birthday at Spookie the Clown's Halls of Pizza, mysteriously disappeared . . ."

I dropped the book on my lap. My birthday! My name!

My pulse quickened and I stifled a scream. *Calm down, Mac. Don't get Mom and Dad racing up here. Your imagination is in overdrive. You didn't really read what you thought you just read.*

I returned to where I had left off.

"Witnesses to the event reported strange occurrences. Barry Lennon, the best friend of MacKenzie

Griffin, reported that a gray ghostlike being had cornered young MacKenzie in the basement."

I sat up straight against the headboard of the bed. Beads of perspiration broke out on my forehead.

"'I closed my eyes out of fear,'" Barry reported. 'When I opened them again, MacKenzie was gone.' MacKenzie Griffin was never found . . ."

Tears welled in my eyes. I could not explain what was happening.

Either I was going crazy, or this was some kind of phantom book that predicted the future.

If the latter was correct, I was a goner.

A piercing wail shattered the silence in my room. I bolted upright in my bed. The back of my pajama shirt was soaked with sweat. The shirt stuck to my skin.

Outside the wail grew fainter. It sounded as if it came from somewhere on the street behind our house.

My mind cleared, and I recognized the sound as an ambulance siren. I rubbed my eyes.

Unbelievable! I had fallen asleep and had dreamed I was reading the account of my birthday disappearance.

Either Mom or Dad had turned off my reading lamp before going to bed. I turned it on again and reached for the book, which lay on the floor.

I opened the book and scanned chapter thirteen. Sure enough. No mention of my birthday party. In fact, the last event reported in the book happened in 1990.

I placed the book on my bedside table, turned out the light, and crawled back under the covers. I prayed I wouldn't dream any more that night.

On awaking the next morning, my hopes for the day were that lunch, school, homework, and sleeping would be more sane than last night's dream. I really needed to get my imagination under control.

After breakfast, I gathered up my horror book collection and headed for school. Several of us who were forming the new horror story book club entered the library together. The lights were on, but no librarian was in sight. We sat down at the largest table.

I placed my collection in front of me. The others did the same. I looked over the stack next to mine. Some series had more than forty books in them. One kid brought a series for little kids called Boo! Books.

While we waited for the librarian to come and lead our meeting, I said, "It looks like there are dozens of horror series. I'm not sure that I've read many books in any of them. Maybe we need to do a short review on each series before we talk about the books."

A girl from my math class spoke next. "I thought they were all the same. Aren't they all about ghosts or monsters? I like to read them because they scare me."

The girl next to her interjected, "I don't think so. My favorite group of books has a historical background."

"And mine comes three stories to a book," another said.

"One series I have is more about ghosts than monsters and another is about a street called Scare Avenue," the boy across from me said.

"The series I brought has endings that will shock you. They've actually helped me deal with my fears," I told them.

The boy across from me was just opening his mouth to say something when the doors to the library flew open. I whipped my head around and expected to see the librarian. I didn't.

In the library's doorway stood a ghost that looked as if it had just walked out of a grave.

7

All of us jumped up from our seats and moved to the farthest point away from the ghostly creature. It turned our way. It stared at us and moaned. Then it moved directly toward us.

I felt my heart beating in my throat. I had hoped that this day would be uneventful. That hope was shot already.

All of us spread out along the back wall. The ghost would be able to grab one of us but not all of us. Someone would be able to get away. The refugee from the graveyard took a few more steps and twisted its dead-looking head toward the table with our books spread on it.

The books diverted the ghost's attention. It walked to a chair, pulled it out, and sat down. It reached out and grabbed one of the books from my stack and flipped it open.

We were in shock as we watched the walking dead become the reading dead. It turned, stared at us, and spoke for the first time. "Books good. Me read. Become member of club."

I stepped forward and started stammering in an attempt to talk to the creature.

It looked at me and said, "Mr. Griffin, you can get your cohorts and sit down. If I am going to lead this group, we need to get going before my first class arrives."

It was the librarian. I think we were more shocked that a school librarian would do something so cool than when the ghost entered.

"I can't believe it's you," I said. "Can I ask why you did it?"

"MacKenzie, I dressed up like this because I wanted all of you to have a real experience that you can carry to your books. When you read them, remember what you felt a few minutes ago. It will make them come to life," she answered.

I didn't need her entrance to remind me of feeling scared. I had pizza ghosts, raincoats, trees, smiley faces, and crepe paper to remember my feelings of mouth-drying fear.

"It was really cool," one of the others said.

"It was nothing. You should see what I do when kids read books about the ocean. Sea monsters are tough costumes to find, and seaweed isn't easy to clean up," she said as she smiled.

We gathered around her. She thought our idea

about a review of the different series would be good. We talked about who would do theirs at the next meeting. The class bell rang, and I was out the door to start my classes.

The day passed quickly. Even soccer practice breezed by. When I walked out of the gym door into the late afternoon sun, I saw Lisa waiting for me underneath the big elm tree.

"What's going on? Why are you still here?" I quizzed.

Usually, Lisa and Frankie go to the library or to each other's houses after school. I felt uneasy when I saw Lisa. Her face gave me a reason to be concerned.

"It's Davis," Lisa answered with a troubled tone. Her eyes looked as if she was frightened by something.

"What happened to Davis? Did he get hurt or something?" My words popped out of my mouth as I moved close to her.

"He is all right now, but in a few minutes he may not be," Lisa said.

I was confused. So far, she had told me nothing, but she had managed to frighten me a lot. With frustration in my voice I said, "Tell me what's going on. The suspense has to be worse than whatever is happening."

"Frankie, Davis, and I were helping the biology teacher with something, and Davis started asking lots of questions about Spookie's place.

"We told him what we read in that library book

yesterday, and he decided to have a look for himself. He left about ten minutes ago and was heading for that old building," Lisa stated.

"So, he'll walk by it, and it will look like a pizza place for little kids. Then he'll go home. What's the big deal?" I said to calm her fears for our friend, though my stomach was growing queasy with nervousness as I spoke.

"That isn't exactly what he planned," Lisa continued. "He said that he is going to disprove the legend before the party. He plans on going down there and trying to get in."

"I don't think there is anything to worry about," I said, trying to sound convincing to both Lisa and myself.

Lisa looked at me hard and said, "You're not listening to me, Mac. Davis plans on going around to the back of the building and sneaking inside. What if the ghosts capture him? No one would know for sure what happened. I told him it was a dumb idea, but Davis is trying hard to be a part of our group. Sometimes, like this time, I think he tries too hard."

My thoughts were racing. Surely, Davis would be safe in broad daylight. And the restaurant workers would be there. And all the stories about ghosts were just fiction, weren't they?

But what about the people I had read about—the people who had witnessed the apparitions, the bakery custodian who had been attacked by a ghost? What if the restaurant staff thought he was a burglar?

"We've got to get down there and stop him from going inside. Hurry," I said. I bolted past Lisa in the direction of Spookie the Clown's Halls of Pizza.

It was only a few blocks from the school, and with a fast walk we could be there in five minutes. The problem was that Davis was already there. He really could be in the hands of ghosts for all I knew.

We reached the building and stopped abruptly in front of it. I stared at the old, rough red-brick front. A large mural was painted above the front door with an enormous clown's face. Out of his mouth was a painted dialogue balloon like in comic books. Spookie was saying, "Spookie the Clown's Halls of Pizza is a killer-fun place."

That was all I needed to see. I turned to Lisa and said, "Davis may already be inside. We need to do something quick to save him."

I walked up to the front door of the haunted building. I planned to yank the door open, rush inside, and get my friend back. Lisa was right behind me.

My palms were so sweaty that I needed to wipe them on my jeans before gripping the door handle. I reached out and grabbed it. I looked at Lisa. I looked at the handle one more time and breathed in a long, hard breath as I yanked.

"I think it's locked," I told her.

"Are you sure it isn't stuck?" Lisa asked.

I yanked again and turned to her saying, "It's definitely locked. He must have gotten in some other way."

Stepping back from the building, I examined the options that Davis might have taken. To the left of the building was a narrow alley that led to the back of the building.

Lisa looked at me with wide, frightened eyes and said, "He had planned to go in the back door, so that alley must be the direction he went. We better find out."

"No, both of us can't go. You stay here and be the lookout. I'm going back there," I told her.

I was scared to go by myself. I really wanted Lisa to be with me, but I knew that my plan made the most sense. I had to go down that dark alley by myself. I knew it, but I didn't like it.

As I moved slowly down the narrow corridor, I wanted to sing or whistle. But if I was going to rescue Davis from ghosts—real or imaginary, it didn't matter—I couldn't make any noise. I had to settle for a silent prayer.

At the end of the alley I found myself in a narrow street that ran between the city buildings. The stores and restaurants kept their garbage cans back there and out of sight.

I moved to my right in the direction of Spookie's

back door. Each step brought me closer, but my legs were heavy and my feet fought me when I moved them forward. I didn't want to get close to the back door, but my friend's health depended on it.

When I was only inches from the door, I heard someone turn the knob. My eyes darted all around for a place to hide. I was about a foot from some garbage cans. I made one big leap and ducked down behind them.

The figure moved out of the back door and went to the garbage Dumpster on the other side of the entrance. I heard two large bags dropped into it. In another few seconds, the back door closed.

I sighed and started to stand up, but one foot slipped on a banana peel and I dropped to the alley's cement. I would have laughed at how funny it was to slip on a banana peel, but my hand dropped on top of something. There underneath my fingers was Davis's prized Pittsburgh Pirates baseball cap.

My heart was beating fast. I was getting dizzy thinking that Davis was inside with phantoms.

It took me a moment to catch my breath and to stand up. I raced down the alley to the front of the building with Davis's cap in my hand.

When I shot out of the alley, Lisa looked over at me and then at the hat in my hands. She threw her hands to her mouth and let out a groan of fear. She took a step back from me and grabbed on to a streetlight. I think Lisa felt the same dizziness that I had.

"I found this by the back door. Davis is inside, and we've got to help him," I told her.

"What can we do?" Lisa asked while holding even tighter to the pole.

"Let's go home. I'll call Barry, and you call Frankie. We need every one of our crew to come back tonight. We'll sneak in and save him. Plan to meet me here at ten o'clock," I said. Yes, I was actually planning to sneak out of my house—and was encouraging my friends to do the same. I had never done such a thing before and probably wouldn't have this time, but I really believed Davis was in trouble.

We ran to our houses. I crashed through the front door and dropped my bag by the staircase. My hand was on the phone before I heard the backpack hit the floor. "Hi, Barry. This is Mac. I don't have time to explain right now, but somebody's got Davis. Ask your parents if you can sleep over so we can get into Spookie's to help him."

Barry said okay and was off the phone. I nearly ran into the kitchen where Dad was cooking dinner. "Dad, can Barry sleep over tonight?" I asked.

"Hey, is that any way to greet your old dad, especially when he is sweating over a hot stove?" He grinned at me as he said it.

"Sorry. Hi, Dad. Now, can Barry sleep over?"

He looked at me and scrunched up his eyebrows while he shook his head. "I guess so. Why don't you go wash your hands and call your mother? She is at her office."

I tried to stay quiet during dinner. I didn't want them to know what was going on. I had gotten Davis into this mess, and I had to get him out—or so I thought.

As I was rinsing off the last dish from dinner, the front doorbell rang. The next thing I knew, Barry was standing next to me with an intensely worried look on his face. He asked, "What's going on, Mac?"

I told him about the book, the legend of the clowns, the treasure, and what Davis had planned on doing. Then I pulled Davis's Pirates cap from my back pocket. I told him how I had found the cap behind the haunted pizza place.

He said very little. Barry was not often without anything to say. When I finished, he said, "So, what's the plan?"

"We've got to break in there tonight. We're going to meet Frankie and Lisa at ten o'clock. Once we're inside we'll split into pairs and search for Davis," I answered.

After I finished putting the dishes in the dishwasher, Barry and I headed upstairs to do our homework. We were almost to the top step when the phone rang. My mom answered it.

We listened closely but couldn't hear all of what Mom was saying until she said, "Sure, let me call him to the phone. I'm sure that he can help you out."

Barry's eyes looked like two big moons orbiting his head. I'm sure I had the same fearful look moving across my quickly warming face.

"MacKenzie, the phone is for you."

"See if I can call them back, Mom. Barry and I are really busy," I responded.

"Mac, it's Davis Wong. He says that he needs your help desperately," she said.

My legs began to wobble. I had to sit down.

"Are you going to get it upstairs, Mac?" Mom asked.

"Yes, I'll get it in my room."

Barry and I raced down the hall and into my room. I snatched up the phone and said, "I've got it, Mom."

I waited for her to hang up and whispered into the phone, "Davis, this is Mac. I know where you are, and we're planning to get you out of there at ten tonight."

"What?" Davis responded. "I'm at home watching TV. Why would I want you to get me out of my house?"

"Well, I thought that . . . oh, never mind." I had a big smile of relief on my face. So Barry would know what was going on, I said, "How did you get out?"

"Out of what? Mac, what happened? Did you get hit on the head in soccer tonight?" he quizzed.

"Didn't you go to Spookie's after school?"

Davis laughed and responded, "Sure, and that's why I'm calling. I went down the alley next to it and found the back door. I was going to sneak in, but someone came outside to throw away garbage, and I ran out of there. The only trouble is that I dropped my cap in that alley. I was wondering if you could go with me before school to look for it."

"Davis, I'll do even better than that. I went looking for you and found the Pirates cap. I'll bring it to school tomorrow," I answered.

Barry was almost shaking as I got off the phone. He wanted to know what had happened. After I told him, I called Frankie and Lisa to tell them the relieving news.

Afterward, Barry and I worked on our homework for a little while. Then I dug out my video game and we went for the highest score. I thought that since I had the home court advantage, I would win. I should have known better. Video games were Barry's thing. He cleaned my clock on every one of them.

"How do you do that? Do you practice every day?" I quizzed.

"If you have to know, yes, I do practice every day, but I also seem to have a gift for it," he answered.

"I don't think there is such a gift or talent called Video Game," I challenged.

"No, that isn't the way I mean it. It takes a degree of concentration and eye-to-hand coordination. I just do these things well," he said. Then he sat back against the foot of the bed. I could tell he was thinking deeply about something.

41

"What are you thinking about?" I asked.

"I'm scared," he said.

"Scared that I'll beat you so badly that you won't be able to show your face at school?" I asked jokingly.

"I'm scared of ghosts. Do you really think that they exist?" he asked.

I sat back against the bed too. "Well, I do know that Ephesians 6:12 says 'We are fighting against the rulers and authorities and the powers of this world's darkness.' And that God's Spirit is greater than the darkness. So I guess that if there *are* ghosts there's really nothing to be afraid of."

We sat quietly until the wind moved a branch, and it brushed against my window. "Did you hear that?"

"It was just the wind, I think," he answered.

Funny how I could quote Scripture and then be spooked not a minute later. I could feel my imagination starting to run away with even the smallest things. I was getting tired, and that always happened when I got tired. "I think we better hit the hay," I told him.

"Hit the what?" His eyebrows crunched down, showing his confusion.

"Hit the hay. It means go to bed," I told him. I thought everyone used the expression.

"Why does it mean that? Where in the world did that expression come from?" Barry pondered.

"Listen, I've already used up all my brain power on

the plan to free Davis. Let's get some sleep and ask someone else in the morning."

We laughed and crawled off to bed. Mom and Dad had two beds in my room, so I could have friends over. I think Barry used that bed more than anyone else I knew.

I had just started to drift off to sleep when I heard a strange noise outside. I thought it might be the branch against the window again, but the next time I heard it, I could tell that it was coming from the backyard.

I slipped out of bed and shook Barry, but he was already awake.

"Hey, did you hear that?" I asked. "I heard the same thing yesterday when I was coming home from the library."

"Yes, I heard it around my house last night," he answered. "My mom heard it and sent my dad out to see what caused it. He didn't find anything. If we could find the reason behind the noise, my mom would sleep a whole lot better. Let's check it out. Or do you think it might be the ghosts?"

I gave him my don't-be-ridiculous look, and we slipped out of our beds. I opened the door slowly to make sure that my parents were already in bed. It was quiet and dark downstairs.

I crept down the stairs as Barry stayed close behind me. We tiptoed past Mom and Dad's bedroom door and into the kitchen. My hand twisted the knob and pulled the door open. The two of us slipped into the dark night.

"Where do you think it came from?" my best friend whispered.

"I couldn't tell, but let's try near the garbage cans," I told him. We never got there. I had no more than finished my statement when we heard a noise. We whipped our heads in the direction of the garage.

Barry put his finger to his lips as an instruction to keep silent. With his other hand, he pointed at the garage. We slid softly through the wet grass. I could not see a thing by the small building.

As we got closer, something shifted inside the large bush in front of us. We looked at each other and I gulped. I thought, *Is it really a ghost? Is it one of the 'powers of this world's darkness'?*

Another four steps put us next to the big bush. I couldn't see anything. I was looking down at the ground when Barry let out a howl. I looked up in enough time to see a dark form leaping at Barry's head from the bush.

Barry dived for the ground as the flying dark, ghostly figure propelled itself toward his head. It missed him by only two inches, but it didn't miss me.

The flying ghost of the night slammed into my chest. I cried out, "Ahh! Get it off me!"

I twisted and turned in a wild attempt to free myself from the sharp claws of the phantom visitor. I finally grabbed its head, and the ghost said, "Meow."

A black cat dropped to the wet grass by my feet and shot off into the night. Barry had rolled over and saw the terror that went through my eyes and body. Then he saw the cat and cracked up.

"Did the little kitty scare you?" he said.

"At least I stood my ground and stayed on my feet," I fired back.

He laughed, and that caused me to break out in giggles. "I guess it was nothing. We better get back to bed before Mom and Dad discover our little adventure."

We didn't say anything as we crossed the lawn and

climbed the back porch steps. As I pulled the screen door open, a sinking feeling hit my stomach. I had forgotten to turn the button to keep the door from locking behind us.

I grabbed the knob and tried twisting it. Nothing happened. We were locked out.

"I've got some bad news for us," I told my friend. "We are locked out of the house."

"Then we'll just go around to the front door and ring the bell. Your dad will open the door, and we'll all go back to bed," he answered as if that action would have no repercussions on my intimate family relationships.

"Barry, I've got a tough enough time convincing them that I'm not a little kid. If they find out that I did something stupid like this, I'll be grounded until I have a full beard that reaches my navel."

"How about a window?" he suggested.

"That is a good idea. The one into Dad's workroom is usually open. He likes lots of fresh air. I'll bet he didn't lock it the last time he was in there," I said as I ran around to the side of the house.

The window was wide open. I bent over to inspect it. By then Barry was standing behind me. "I don't think we are the first ones to use this window to get in."

"Maybe my other idea was better. Let's go around front and ring the bell," he suggested strongly.

I lay down flat on the ground. Actually, it wasn't on the ground. It was right on top of Dad's prize flowers. I attempted to move them out of the way, but a good bed of flowers is too thick to move. I would have to tell my parents the whole story the next day.

I wiggled my body in through the window. The workbench was below the window. The drop was short, but Dad had left a glass jar of nuts and bolts near the edge. In the dark, I bumped them.

Nothing I did could stop their suicide leap to the floor. The crash sent shivers through me.

I tried to keep Barry from knocking anything else off the bench. His foot struck a mallet, and it toppled off. I could barely see it as my hand shot into the darkness to retrieve it. I was lucky and snatched it out of the air.

We stood in the workroom. "The rec room is on the other side of this door. If any ghouls got in here before us, they are waiting for us in there," I said in a very low whisper.

"Do you think that they got in so they could play foosball?" Barry joked.

I ignored him and went to open the door. Before my hand could reach the knob, I heard movements on the other side.

"What should we do?" Barry asked.

"I don't know. Maybe we should grab a hammer and go after it," I answered.

"We won't have to go after it. It's coming to us!" Barry said with panic as he watched the knob turn slowly.

11

The door flew open.

"DAD!" I screamed as he raised a baseball bat in the air.

He reached over and flipped on the light. He stared at us with narrowed, squinting eyes and didn't say a word. That meant he was really angry. He sucked in a deep breath and set the bat down.

"Could you please explain to me why you are sneaking into a window of your own house? And while you're at that, could you add an explanation of why you were outside in the first place? And don't you realize that it's dangerous breaking into a house?" he asked with his anger rising on each question.

"It was really stupid, Mr. Griffin, but it was my idea." Barry attempted to take the blame.

"Barry, I'm really to blame. This is my house. I knew the rules, and I broke them. Dad, I'm sorry. We heard that strange noise, and we slipped outside to see what it was. Instead of finding the walking dead strolling around in the garden, your adventurous son locked himself out of the house."

"You heard it too?" Dad said with interest. He seemed to forget he was mad at us. He totally refocused on the mysterious noise. "Did you see anything?"

"We thought we saw something by the garage. When we went over there, a cat jumped on me."

"I have a suggestion. Why don't we sleep on all this and talk about the vicious kitty that attacks kids in the morning after we've rested?" Dad said.

As we walked upstairs, my dad told us, "You two better get to bed. Sleep in an extra fifteen minutes, and I'll drive you to school."

When morning came, I expected crazy things to happen at school after all the excitement of the last few days, but it was rather dull until lunchtime.

Barry and I were describing how we confronted a horrible ghoul in my backyard. I liked his version. We were much braver than the actual fact.

Frankie looked us right in the eyes and said, "I don't believe this story."

"It's true," Barry defended.

"Most of it is true," I added.

"Which part is true?" Davis asked.

"We did see a mysterious, dark shape that looked like a ghost in the backyard," I answered.

"I saw a ghost in my pajamas once," Davis said

with a smile. "What he was doing in my pajamas, I'll never know."

Frankie and Lisa thought it was an extremely funny joke and nearly fell from the cafeteria seats because they were laughing so hard. Barry and I were not amused.

I opened my lunch bag and pulled out my sandwich. When I unwrapped it, the bread had "Happy Birthday Almost" on it, written in mustard. As I said, Mom was crazy sometimes.

"Cute, really cute," Frankie said. "I can't wait to see what the rest of your lunch looks like."

Lucky for me that there were no more embarrassing food items. In fact, the rest of that school day had no embarrassing moments.

Before I went into the house, I checked the area where I saw the cat by the garage in case I had missed something. Nothing was there. Next, I inspected the window by Dad's workroom to assure myself that nothing could get in.

Once in the house, I discovered that Mom and Dad were still at work. I looked around for any sign of ghosts. There was nothing. I was starting to get paranoid. It was crazy to think that ghosts would be lurking around my house and waiting for me. It was crazy, but I was still glad nothing was there. I needed to think less about ghosts and more about the protector *against* ghosts.

For the rest of the night I watched TV and did my homework, sometimes at the same time. I had been trying to convince my parents that it helps me concentrate. I've even read articles to them about kids with attention disorders who were helped by keeping a TV on. They haven't bought it.

Even my dreams were filled with nothing special. I got up the next morning, showered, and dressed. I was pulling on my Dodgers cap when I stepped into the kitchen. At my place setting was a plate of pancakes nearly a foot high, and on top of them burned twelve candles.

My parents leaped out from behind the kitchen counter. "Happy Birthday!" they yelled.

"Thanks, Mom and Dad. I can't believe that I'm twelve, almost a full-grown man." I threw that in as a hint to my mother.

"You better hurry and blow out the candles," Dad said.

"Okay, Lord, please let my party tonight be the talk of the school on Monday." With that I puffed out the candles with a single blow.

The pancakes were great and I was only halfway through when Barry showed up at the back door for us to walk to school together.

"Wow!" he said as he peeked through the screen door. "That is the biggest pile of pancakes that I have ever seen."

"You know how it is when you're the birthday boy," I kidded. I took a few more bites and grabbed my backpack, and we were on our way to school.

It was a quiet morning. I knew that lunch wouldn't be as quiet. That night was the birthday party at Spookie the Clown's. That night we would probably meet up with whatever was haunting that building.

I walked into the cafeteria and slipped into my seat at our table. Barry and Frankie arrived next from their class together. Lisa was going through the lunch line along with Davis.

Davis had to eat the cafeteria food. Since his dad was the vice principal, he had to eat the mysterious food substances they served to show his belief that the food was okay. It wasn't.

"How are the party plans for tonight, MacKenzie?" Frankie asked.

"Just about every kid who was invited is coming. To tell you the truth, after all the weird things that happened this week, I have a strange feeling that tonight will be the weirdest time of my life," I told the others.

Lisa agreed, but Frankie was unsure that it would be scary. She told us, "A girl in my English class said her little brother had a party there last week and nothing strange happened. No one saw a ghost. No one saw any type of ghoul, apparition, or floating phantom. I think we're all getting a little carried away with the ghost at Spookie the Clown's Halls of Pizza."

52

Davis interrupted and said, "I heard just the opposite. A couple of guys from gym class said they heard that it was haunted and that two kids disappeared there last week. The police don't want to panic people, so it hasn't been in the newspaper."

"It doesn't matter what other kids are saying. Tonight, we all find out for ourselves," Barry told us.

I opened my lunch bag and pulled out my sandwich. I dumped out the apple with no brown spots. I hate brown spots. Next came a bag of chips. From the bottom of the paper sack came a brightly wrapped gift. The others looked at me.

"Open it," Frankie urged.

"Mom didn't say anything about a birthday gift in my lunch bag. How do I know it's from her? It could have been put in here by anybody, including the mysterious ghosts at Spookie's," I kidded, using my best scary voice.

I took the bow off. "Well, nothing happened—so far."

I undid a piece of tape on the bottom. "It still didn't blow up," I joked some more.

Next, I pulled the Happy Birthday wrapping paper from around the small box. "Nothing unusual," I said, stretching out the suspense.

"Well, are you going to open it or not?" Frankie asked.

"Would you if some ghosts had wrapped it and sneaked it into your lunch bag?" Lisa said.

I wasn't sure if she was kidding or not.

"Of course, if some loving, caring ghosts took all that time to wrap a nice gift to make my birthday a little brighter, I would open it a lot faster than you are," she said and then started laughing.

I pulled the top off. "Oh, no!" I gasped and dropped the box.

"HAPPY BIRTHDAY! HAPPY BIRTHDAY! HAPPY BIRTHDAY! HAPPY BIRTHDAY! HAPPY BIRTH-DAY! HAPPY BIRTHDAY! HAPPY BIRTHDAY!" a computer chip blared.

The entire cafeteria was standing up. Some kids had even climbed on tables to see what was going on.

I didn't know what to do. I had dropped the lid on the floor and couldn't find it. Replacing it might have stopped the sound, but I couldn't see it under the table. Actually, I wanted to stay under the table. Then the sound stopped as suddenly as it began.

I pulled my head up from under the table and found myself the focus of a roomful of stares. I smiled. No one said a word.

I wanted to jump up and run out of the cafeteria. I was embarrassed, but I also thought it was funny. I looked back at the other kids and asked, "Does any-one else have a gift for me?" They laughed and went back to their lunches.

After school, I hurried home to tell Mom about the havoc she caused, but she was gone. She left a note on the fridge that said she went shopping for party favors. I could see her carrying in her brightly colored little bags with plastic whistles, squirt guns, and pretend watches. I shook my head and decided to shoot some hoops to burn off some of my pre-birthday-party excitement.

I was hitting my shots one after another. It was nothing but net. I was so into it that the next thing I knew, Mom was calling my name, "MacKenzie, we need to go, or you'll be late for your own birthday party."

I rolled the ball into the garage and headed for the minivan. Mom was already throwing things for the party into the back. I kept telling her that since I was an only child, she could get a car that was a little sportier. So she got a *red* minivan.

She picked up Barry, Davis, Frankie, and Lisa. The other kids from school and church had gotten there on their own. My party consisted of three different groups. There were the guys I played soccer with, my friends in the van with me, and a small group from my church youth group.

Mom squealed her wheels to a stop in front of Spookie's. A bunch of little kids were leaving the Halls of Pizza. They had bright helium balloons stringing from their wrists and traditional birthday bags of goodies in their hands.

I sighed. None of them looked scared, so it must really be a little kids' place. I wouldn't be able to show my face at school, practice, or church. How much fun could Spookie's be for a bunch of middle schoolers if little kids liked it so much? *This is going to be a drag*, I thought.

We all jumped out. I had taken only a few steps from the minivan when Davis grabbed me and pulled my body to a halt. "Afraid to go in?" I asked. "Are you afraid that you'll lose at Pin the Tail on the Donkey?"

"No, that isn't it. I read something in the newspaper about this place," he said seriously.

"So?"

"This building really is haunted. It's like the Bermuda Triangle of our town. Strange things happen here. The article talked about the last business to go under and the one before that. I asked my dad about it, and he said there are ghosts here looking for hidden treasure. All that happens is the work of those ghosts," he whispered.

"That's the legend," I told him. "I read about it in a book the other night."

"I'm not sure that I want to go in, but I'm not staying out here by myself," he finished and we walked in.

The rest of the kids were already waiting in the Halls of Pizza foyer. The foyer's walls were covered with all kinds of crazy things. It looked a lot cooler than I thought it would.

Right above the door was a stuffed head of Spookie. It looked like one of those moose heads people hang on their walls.

I nudged Davis and said, "Tough place. They even stuff the heads of the past Spookies. Or do you think the ghosts did that to him?"

Frankie tipped her face in next to ours, pointed up at the stuffed heads on the wall, and said, "My dad wants one of those with a purple dinosaur on it."

Davis and I cracked up. It helped me to forget what Davis had reminded me of.

We were making jokes about the clown's head when it suddenly opened its eyes and yelled, "Welcome to Spookie the Clown's Halls of Pizza."

I jumped backward and nearly knocked Lisa over. I heard the others let out gasps and eeks. My heart leaped into my mouth, and I felt totally speechless.

Spookie pulled his head out of the hole and dropped down to the other side of the door with a thump and opened it. "Hey, kids. Welcome to my Halls of Pizza. Are you ready to have a fun and crazy evening with us? We've got some really wacky games and loony prizes. Ho, hey, ho! This is going to be one funnnn night!"

When he finished, I rolled my eyes and shot a glance at the others. "I knew it was really him all the time," I told them.

Frankie and Lisa giggled. I guess the two of them didn't believe me.

Spookie grabbed my arm and ushered me and all my friends through the door. I was shocked when we got inside. The place was enormous. There were doors to Halls of this and Halls of that. I heard the video games beeping, whirring, gasping, and dinging only a few feet away.

At least the game time of the party sounded fun. I just hoped that Spookie and his clown team of pizza makers and waitpersons wouldn't have us sing little kids' songs or play baby games. If they did, I was going to crawl under the table and not come out until I graduated from middle school.

Spookie spun around, clapped his hands together, and said, "Boys and girls, could I have your attention?"

All of us groaned in unison.

"Oops, did I say something wrong? You know Spookie, just kidding around. Anyway, children, let's head into the party room."

We groaned together one more time and fell in behind the clown corps. The party room looked like a carnival midway. Games were all along the sides of the room, and tables filled the middle.

Spookie went all out for his place. Even the electronic animated characters standing by the midway games looked real. Of course, in the blinking, colored lights almost anything could have looked real. They cast an odd glow across the games and my friends.

I wandered around looking at things. Most of the others were doing the same thing. Spookie's workers pushed chairs and tables into place while the electronic characters sang and danced.

In a dark corner, far from the entrance, was a group of electronic kids playing the old children's game Ring Around the Rosy. They moved their circle around a figure in the middle. From the distance, in the crazily lighted room, the figure looked like a dingy gray sheet that was hung on a line.

I walked closer to get a better look. Once again, my curiosity got the better of me. I kept thinking that I needed to stay with the others, but the circling kids seemed to be drawing me toward them. I got closer but still couldn't see what the gray form was.

At five feet away, I looked into the eyes of the center figure. It wore a baggy clown costume, but it wasn't colored like one. Instead, everything, including the clown's makeup, was gray. It sent a shiver up my spine. When it reached my brain, my body stiffened. Could it be one of the ghosts that haunted the Tremble Avenue building?

I shook my head to shake that frightening thought loose, then took a step back. On the second backward step, I bumped into something. It must have been one of the clowns.

Before I could say anything, the being behind me spoke. "Do you know what the legend is behind that scene?"

I tried to turn around, but two hands gripped my shoulders, holding me still. "Come now. Do you know where we got that little rhyming game?"

Without looking back I said, "No, sir. I came over to see what was in the middle of the circle and . . ."

The person behind me didn't wait for me to answer. He said, "When England was struck with the plague hundreds of years ago, they thought the dirty air was killing them. So, they filled their pockets with flowers and walked around with handfuls of posies up to their noses. Don't you think that it's silly to try to protect yourself with a handful of flowers?" He dropped his hands from my shoulders.

I tried to be polite, but the truth was that I was frightened so badly that my teeth were chattering and I was too scared to turn around. I tried to speak, but my voice came out in a high pitch. "Thank you for telling me that. I guess you want me to join the others for the party?"

No response. I spun around. No one was there. Where did he go? Or was he a he? I was really starting to buy into this ghost business. Maybe I had just met one of them.

I didn't want to hang around and find out. I shot back toward my friends.

The others had already taken seats. A large red velvet chair at the end of the table was empty. I figured it was for me when Barry and Davis waved me over to it. They were sitting on either side of my birthday throne. Frankie and Lisa were next to them, and then the others merged into their groups.

Barry was trying to talk to me as I sat down, but the old-time organ music was so loud that I couldn't hear him. I was trying to yell in his ear that I met a ghost, but the music grew louder.

The music didn't stop until Spookie stood in the center of us and clapped his hands. It was obvious that he was the clown in charge.

"Throughout the night, you will be moved to different areas to do different activities. I see that we can split you easily into groups of five. Sometimes one group will be one place while the others are someplace else. Don't worry. We all end up at the same place when the party ends," he explained.

"That is, if the ghosts of the building don't get us first," Barry tossed in.

"That's what I was trying to tell you. I went over to see what that gray figure was in the middle of the kids playing Ring Around the Rosy, and a ghost grabbed me," I told him excitedly.

Barry looked at me and then at the display. He looked back at me and asked, "What did the ghost look like?"

"I don't know. He grabbed me from behind, and when I turned around, he was gone. But he told me about some weird legend behind the kids' Ring Around the Rosy game. I was scared," I told him in a loud whisper.

He scrunched his eyebrows together as if he was

questioning my sanity. But before he could speak, the waiters and waitresses were swarming around us with plates and glasses.

I thought it was unusual that their faces weren't happy clown faces. Each one looked more like a demented or twisted monster face. As my waitress reached over my shoulder to set down a glass, I got a good look at her. Her clown makeup covered a mass of distorted flesh. She looked right at me and snarled.

For a second I thought that maybe Spookie's wasn't just for little kids. Maybe it was going to be too much for me, even if I was twelve.

Since Barry was doubting my ability to see correctly, I leaned over to Davis to ask if he had gotten a good look at the waitress's face. "Hey, did you see that? I don't think she's . . ."

CRASH! The wall across from us blew apart in a puff of smoke, sending parts of stone into the air. As the air cleared, I heard a horn beep, and then I saw it. A car had come through the wall and was rolling toward our table.

14.

All five of us dived for the floor as the car's clown-faced driver screeched her tires in a wild attempt to stop the almost cartoonish-looking auto. The clown's eyes were wide with what looked like terror.

I don't know if it was terror that she would hit us or terror that she wouldn't hit us. No matter what, the five of us were on the floor looking at a car headed our way.

"What's going on?" Davis asked.

Lisa looked shocked. She screamed, "We've got to get out of here. It's still coming right at us."

The five of us scrambled to the back wall until we could not move any farther.

"Sorry. I guess my birthday party will be everybody's last one," I told them, but I don't think they heard me because of the screeching tires on the automobile.

The clown driver jumped out of her seat and yelled, "Howdy, am I late for the party?"

Spookie was rolling with laughter across the top of one of the tables. He could barely get the words out, "Look, kids! It's Penny the Party Crasher."

She had come through a fake wall built out of plastic blocks. By the time I got a good look at it, the other clown helpers were pushing it back into place.

Penny was bouncing from table to table doing silly magic tricks. She had not arrived at our table because we hadn't gotten back in our seats yet. Davis pulled me up, and we pulled the other three up. My friends and I slumped our shoulders and walked embarrassedly back to our party seats and began eating our pizza.

"Did I scare you kids?" she asked.

"No, and we're not kids," I answered. I didn't want to give her the satisfaction of knowing that I couldn't tell if it was my heart or my tongue in my mouth.

She reached her white-gloved hand over and tousled my hair. Then Penny reached behind my ear and pulled out some coins. She dropped them on the table, but they just kept pouring out. Hundreds fell before us as she giggled.

"Well, birthday boy, you really should clean your ears out more often," Penny told me and my friends. "You had all these tokens for Spookie's Hall of Games stuck behind your eardrum. But I beat them out of you. Get it? Beat them out? Eardrum? Beat drums?"

I understood her joke, but I was still trying to fathom how Penny could think that I believed she got that many coins out of my ear. I must have had a shocked look on my face because Penny snapped her fingers in front of my face.

"Hey, birthday boy, are you still with me?" she asked.

"Oh, yes. That was a really neat trick. Do you think you might look in there and see if there are any handheld video games?" I joked. She smiled and moved away.

Spookie got our attention up front by whistling. "Now that MacKenzie has supplied the tokens, I say let's finish our pizza and get into the Hall of Games for a good time. Try to stay in your groups because we're going to have a big surprise for some of you."

We all ran toward the game room after grabbing a handful of tokens off the table in front of me. I went right to my favorite game, Guardians. The angel-type characters who look like superheroes fight with the bad guys who resemble weird ghouls and ghosts. It's really cool, and they are the same characters that are in my favorite comic book series called Guardians.

Barry and I had all the editions. We battled for the game, but he let me go first because it was my birthday and my favorite game.

I dropped in the tokens and was about to push the

start button when the game began by itself. I wasn't about to waste a second of playing time. I grabbed the joystick and started moving it while I pushed the weapons buttons.

I was racking up lots of points. It seemed that the game was running without me. I laughed at how good I was getting. I was in the video game zone.

Others were crowding around me. Accidentally, Davis was pushed against me, and I lost my grip on the controls. The game continued to play. It was as if something I couldn't see was pushing the joystick from side to front to side to back.

The game was approaching the final level. I had been there only once before because there were so few of the Guardians video games around that I could not practice much. I was afraid to grab back the controls, but I didn't want to frighten the other kids.

I put my hands on the joystick, but I wasn't controlling it. It was working from the inside as if it was haunted. Several of the kids from school cheered as I approached the final round.

I was about to make the highest score in my video game career, but I had absolutely no control over the game. I tried to see where the plug was. Maybe if I unplugged it, the thing would stop. I looked back to the game graphics, and in an instant the screen dissolved and a face slowly formed. It had a grayish tinge and an almost ghostly appearance.

As the picture sharpened, I could see the outline of clown makeup over a distorted, menacing gray face. A handful of long, sharp nails moved up near his face.

He came into crystal-clear view and motioned for me to come closer. Then the machine spoke in a weird computer voice, "Come and play with me. Come closer and play my game, but don't touch my treasure." Then I watched as flower petals dropped from his palm and floated away.

I moved a few steps back.

Barry slipped into my place and said, "Don't quit now. You're almost—ahhhhh!" Barry screamed as he leaped into the air and landed on my feet. I screamed out in pain.

Everyone in the room looked at us. I saw Spookie lean close to Penny's ear and say something that was followed by a snicker. I did not like the looks of that.

I turned back to the Guardians game, and the face had disappeared. All that was left was a frowning yellow circle face with the words, "Delay of game. Sorry but you lose," underneath it. I tried to shake off what I had just witnessed and pulled my group away from the video game.

Barry moved in close to talk so that no one else would hear us. "Did you see what I saw?" I asked.

"Yes, it wasn't what I expected when you got to that level of the game," Barry answered.

"No," I insisted. "I don't think it had anything to do with the game. It was too real looking. It didn't seem computer generated. Besides, I wasn't controlling the game at all. I even took my hands off the joystick, and it continued on its own. I'm not sure I like this place anymore."

"Neither do I, especially after what you said was in that book you read," Barry added. He finished as Frankie and Davis grabbed our arms and yanked us toward a booth called the Game of Life.

Lisa was already standing in front of it. She started instructing us, "According to the directions, we need to get inside the booth and sit down. Then we drop in our tokens and grip the controls in front of us. Sounds easy enough."

I was trying to explain to them what had happened when Barry interrupted me. "Well, after the last one, I could use something a little more sane," he told them.

Lisa pushed my body into the seat. Behind me slid Lisa, Davis, Barry, and Frankie. We were firmly in place when Frankie dropped in her token.

The doors shut quickly, and clamps gripped our hands. We were caught in the Game of Life as it began to flash and groan.

Across from our seats a large curved screen flicked on as loud music poured into our booth. The words *The Game of Life* flashed on the screen. We looked back and forth at one another.

I said to the others, "This doesn't seem like some kind of kids' game to me. Spookie's place is starting to spook me. Barry, maybe we should tell the others."

Frankie said, "Do you two want to tell us how scared you are? Is that what you're trying to say? Relax, this is probably one of those virtual reality rides. It will look and feel as if we're in a roller coaster or a spaceship or something like that."

She was about to say more, but a face popped up on the screen. As the face came into focus, Frankie said, "Look, it's just a clown face. But why is it in black and white?"

I stared at the grayish clown face. "Barry, it's him! It's the face from the Guardians game."

I was sure that the other three wondered what I was talking about, but before anyone could say a thing, the ghostly clown on the computer screen spoke in an eerie, hollow voice: "Welcome to the Game of Life. I'm your host, George Ghouless. Now, let's begin the game. The rules are simple. If you score enough points, we'll open the doors and let you out. And if you don't, we won't."

We all tried to jump out, but our hands were clamped to the controls in front of us. We twisted and pulled, but it was useless.

"What do we do?" Davis asked.

Lisa gave us the harsh reality. "We better answer all the questions right, or we'll end up as eternal members of Spookie's game room."

Our host, George, spoke again, "In the Game of Life, we want to give you a chance. Here are the categories: the History of European Wars, the Mammals of New Zealand, and Obscure Horror Movie Trivia. Which one will it be?"

Barry spoke first. "I don't think we have any choice. We haven't covered European history yet. We barely know where New Zealand is, much less anything about its animals. Right now, I wish that Dracula were here to help us."

"We've got to say which category. Horror Movie Trivia is my choice. What about you guys?" I asked.

In unison they chipped in, "Horror Movie Trivia."

Our computer host said, "Horror Movie Trivia it

will be then. Here is your first question: Who was the Bride of Frankenstein supposed to marry?"

My face beamed. "That's easy. She was made for Frankie himself."

"Correct, children. Let's move to question two. What did Dracula sleep in, and what did it sit on?"

I drew a blank. Frankie and Davis argued something on the other side, but none of us could come up with the answer. The horn buzzed so loud that our teeth rattled.

Our evil video host chimed in, "The answer is: He slept in a coffin that had to sit on dirt from his home in Transylvania. Are you ready for the third question?"

We all shook our heads no, but the question came anyway: "What famous cartoon dog chased ghosts?"

"That one's easy," said Frankie. She broke out in the song, "Scooby-Dooby-Doo, where are you?"

"Correct," George Ghouless told us. "One more correct answer and I'll set you free. Two more incorrect answers and you'll be locked inside forever. And here comes question four: When does a werewolf appear?"

"At night," Barry yelled out.

Before George could say, "Incorrect," the sound of the buzzer stiffened our bodies.

"I think the questions are getting harder," I said to the others. "So, next time, we better really know the answer to the question. By the way, werewolves come out only on a full moon."

Then George said, "Let me see now. I need to make this quiz harder because we have our last question. Answer it right and you'll go free. Answer it wrong and you'll be toast."

"He is a real encouragement," Frankie commented.

Lisa said, "We have to answer this one right."

I could hear panic in the tone of her voice. I realized that she felt the same way that I did.

"Attention!" George commanded. "Question number five is about to be asked." He paused and then proceeded. "What did Dr. Jekyll turn into?"

The ghoul's voice shook us. We all scooted back as far as we could go in our seats. The computer clown ghost was out to win, no matter what.

Barry was getting ready to give an answer when I shot him a glance. "What are our choices?" I yelled at the others.

"A monster," Davis let out as if one was breathing down his neck.

"An evil beast." Lisa's shrill, frightened tone was as scary as George Ghouless.

"Honest, we don't have time to debate this. The clock is ticking, and we have five seconds to give an answer," I pleaded.

Frankie thought for a moment and blurted out, "It's Mr. Hyde."

Suddenly, George broke out in ghoulish laughter. Had we won? Had we lost?

All of us looked at Frankie. She caused our fate. She gave the wrong answer.

George's laugh turned into a sinister computer-generated smile. His white teeth gleamed, and his hand went for the switch. In the next instant the door to our booth slid open, our captive hands were set free, and the seat tipped up, dumping us on the floor.

"Yes, Frankie! You saved us," I cried. "I'll live to see another birthday."

"Nothing to it," she said, but her eyes were distracted from us.

A few feet away, five other guests were entering a booth that was similar to ours. It was called the Game of Chance.

Frankie ran their way, but the five were already inside and the door was sliding shut.

"What should I do?" she said as she turned to the rest of us.

"Have you tried forcing the door open?" Davis asked.

By then Barry and I were standing next to the Game of Chance. We pressed hard on the door and it slid slowly open. I expected to see five surprised faces, but instead, the booth was empty.

"Where did they go?" Barry asked me.

I stuck my head inside but saw no sign of them. I shot my eyes from side to side to see if I could find a trapdoor, but it looked seamless. On the seat were a few flower petals. They were from the posies in the Ring Around the Rosy game.

I turned back to the others. "I don't see how they could have gotten out, but I found these."

Frankie looked confused and said, "We lost some friends and you're worried about some flowers."

I wanted to tell them all the story, but Davis leaned in and said, "We better tell Spookie."

Frankie gave him a hard, long look. "Don't you realize that he is probably behind all this weird stuff? We can't tell Spookie."

The moment she mentioned his name, Spookie's voice blasted out of the speaker above my head. "The Hall of Games is over. Now it is time for the Hall of Food."

Doors opened and we walked into a room that looked like something out of one of those black-and-white 1950s TV shows. The floor was black-and-white squares, and there was an old-fashioned counter with high red stools in front of it. Along the sides of the room were red cushioned booths. One wall was covered with mirrors. Along it stood a tall, thin man with a white paper hat like what a soldier wears.

He greeted us by saying, "Welcome to Big Rick's Cafe. Have a seat. In a few minutes we'll be having—"

Spookie interrupted, "Okay, kids. It's time for cake and ice cream."

I whispered to the others, "He sure is rude. He didn't let the guy from Rick's Cafe speak."

"Who?" Frankie turned to me and asked.

"He is standing right over there." I pointed to where Big Rick had been. Nothing was there. "He was standing right there. He must have left."

Barry gave me a puzzled look and said, "If he did, he would have to walk right through us."

He was right. I must have been seeing things, or I just saw one of the ghosts. "Do you think it could have been a ghost?"

"I think that you're getting delirious from too much pizza. Besides, if a bunch of little tykes could have a party and leave this place unafraid, we should be able to as well," Frankie said.

I was beginning to wonder if anything rattled her.

She could have been right, but I was sure that I saw something. I needed to keep my eyes open to see if that ghost appeared again.

All of us sat at the booths. I looked around for the group that went in the Game of Chance. None of them were with us.

I decided that I needed to talk to Spookie about that, but before I could get his attention, clown waiters and waitresses were swarming all over us with birthday cake and ice cream. It tasted pretty good, and before I knew it, I had forgotten about the other group and the ghost.

"It's time for some party games," Spookie yelled.

"Pin the Tail on the Donkey?" Davis asked. "Oooo! That one really scares me."

"We're going to play Hot Potato. I need you all to get into a circle. This handy little plastic potato winds up and explodes at a certain time. And I mean explodes. Whoever is holding it when it goes off is out of the game. And I mean, really out of the game. That kid may even be out of this world. Does everyone understand?" Spookie instructed. Something about the tone of his voice made me think he truly meant every word he said.

The hot potato flew from one set of hands to another. I was scared of what would happen the first time it exploded. KABOOM! The potato shook, rattled, and blinked, but the excruciatingly loud noise was the worst that happened.

All of our faces went from intense fear to great relief. Hot Potato was only a game.

Within a few minutes most of the others were eliminated, leaving the five in my group. Once Spookie had the five of us standing around the circle, he said, "We need to make this a little more interesting. I'm going to remove the plastic game potato that made a loud noise and replace it with something that will give a real bang."

Spookie pulled from a deep pocket in his baggy clown pants a round, black ball that looked a lot like the bombs in cartoons. "I'm going to set this for a few seconds. The one left holding it when the clock ticks down to zero will probably not hold anything again," the clown said with a sinister snicker.

I looked at Barry, and with my fright showing all over my face I asked, "Do you think that Spookie is trying to get rid of us because he thinks we want the treasure?"

"Maybe he is. It's got to be worth a lot, but I'd rather leave than find it," he answered.

I responded, "I don't see how we can get out." Then I looked up, and Spookie had wound the bomb and tossed it into the hands of Lisa.

She gasped and pitched it into the air toward Davis.

Davis didn't even grab it. He slung it to Barry, who bobbled it because he was yelling at me, "Find a window. Find someplace to throw this out of here."

The little timer read thirteen seconds when Barry

pitched it to Frankie. Frankie's athletic ability came into play. She had the bomb into the air and flying at me with eight seconds showing on the red-lighted timer.

I yelled at Barry, "This can't be happening. A bunch of clowns can't blow up a group of kids and expect to keep their business alive."

Spookie called out to me, "You better concentrate on keeping yourself alive."

He was right, but I started to panic. I needed to grab it and pitch it into a far corner. I reached out as the timer ticked down to three seconds.

The bomb hit my hands, and I froze. I looked for a place to toss it but was too frightened to think quickly. Time had run out. It was all over, and I wouldn't see thirteen.

17

The red light flashed zero. I closed my eyes and waited for the explosion. I waited and waited for the sound of a bang, but instead I heard Spookie laugh. I opened my eyes.

The red light panel was flashing the word *Bang* over and over again. "Really funny," I said to Spookie.

"Oh, come on, birthday boy. Lighten up. We've only just begun. You're getting our best party package, MacKenzie. There is a lot more frightening fun to come.

"Kids, take some seats over there on those steps. The magic show is about to begin," Spookie directed.

As we walked to the other side of the room, several clowns rolled in boxes and props like the ones in the big magic shows on TV. I couldn't believe all that stood in front of us. Spookie the Clown had quite a setup.

In his first trick he put Penny the Party Crasher into a box and sawed her in half. The special effects were great. You couldn't tell how he did it until the whole trick was over, and Penny broke out of the upper half of the box and another clown jumped out of the lower one. The whole place broke into fits of laughter.

"I'm a little embarrassed. It's so hard to find good help these days. Maybe if I used one of you for my next trick, it would turn out better." Spookie barely spoke the words before every hand but mine was up in the air. He laughed and pointed at one of the other kids. The kid was the perfect candidate. He was always joking around, so being on stage was natural to him.

Davis leaned over Frankie and whispered close to my ear. "I'm starting to get a bad feeling. Do you think all the unusual stuff is happening because of the ghosts that haunt this building?"

"What?" I asked because his question startled me. "No, I don't know. I wish I could tell you that it has just been coincidence," I responded as I watched Spookie put our class friend into a box and close the door.

"I will say the magic words, and right before your very eyes, one of your party will disappear," Spookie went on.

Spookie then said the magic words. I wasn't sure what they were. I leaned over to ask Davis what Spookie used as magic words.

He stammered at first and then whispered out in a shrill voice, "I think he said, 'Treasure divine, treasure I'll find, treasure is mine.'"

"Spookie must be working with the ghosts to find the treasure," I said quietly to him. "That's probably why he called himself Spookie. We should have figured that out a long time ago."

I looked up. Spookie opened the box, but instead of our friend, a tall, gray, ghostly clown with bloody fingernails stepped out. It was the figure I saw when we first walked into the Hall of Food. Spookie tried to stop him, but the ghostly clown pushed him away and started moving toward the steps we were sitting on.

The group scattered everywhere while the clowns were flopping behind the figure with their large red-and-yellow clown shoes.

Frankie, Barry, and I made the mistake of moving into a corner. The grayish figure moved slowly in our direction.

"I think I believe the legend completely now," Frankie cried out.

Barry was in total agreement. I could tell by the way his head bobbed up and down.

"What do we do?" I asked.

Frankie quickly came up with a plan. "Everybody go a different way. It might confuse him, and we'll all get free."

It wasn't a perfect plan, but then again it wasn't the perfect little kids' birthday party anymore. I would be glad if I escaped alive.

Barry shot to the right. Frankie shot to the left. I was left with the tough job of getting through the ghostly clown's legs.

I dived for the small opening between his large feet, but he was too quick. Suddenly, I was picked up off the floor and held high in the air until I was face-to-face with what must have been one of the ghosts of the building.

He growled loudly, "Now I've got you, and I guarantee that you won't get what you came for." He squeezed me harder, and I closed my eyes.

There was no escape. I would soon join my friend who had disappeared.

I made the mistake of peeking as he moved me closer with one hand and raised the other hand in the air. I was sure he was going to shove me into his mouth. Instead, the hand moved to the top of his head and pulled off his mask.

"Happy Birthday, MacKenzie," the clown under the ghost mask said. He lowered me to the floor, and I dusted the dirt off my clothes that they picked up in my wild and crazy dive.

"Thanks for the fright," I returned.

"Well, now that all that fun is over, come on back to the steps," Spookie called as my disappearing friend appeared out of a hidden panel in the wall. My friend kept asking, "What happened? What happened?"

I moved back, rather embarrassed that I had let the ghostly clown get the best of me. I wished that I hadn't acted so much like a little kid. Frankie and Barry walked up next to me.

"That was really brave when you dived between

his feet. It really drew his attention away from us. I was sure that we were all goners. This ghost thing has me on edge," Barry said.

"I liked the part where you closed your eyes. I'll bet you were praying," she stated.

"Yes, that would be the best thing to do," I said but I wasn't. Guess I wasn't much of an overcomer. I had been so scared that I didn't think of anything except what they would have to say to my mom. I almost heard Spookie the Clown saying, "Sorry, Mrs. Griffin, but we had a ghost living at our Halls of Pizza, and his favorite game is making birthday boys into toast. We think he took your son, but we would be glad to refund part of your party money."

My imagination came to a close as we reached the stairs and Davis said, "I was so worried that he would eat you." He paused and added, "And then not floss."

I groaned and rolled my eyes.

Frankie put her hand on my shoulder and told us, "That was quite a scare, but it wasn't for real. The ghost wasn't for real. Maybe all the other stuff isn't for real either?"

I wasn't sure, but I didn't want things to get much worse for us.

Spookie said, "Next, kids, we are going to play Hide and Seek."

"It will be more like Hide and Shriek around this place," Davis quipped.

"In a moment, the doors over there will open up,

and you will have three minutes to find a place to hide before 'it' comes to find you," he instructed.

"Does he mean 'it' like 'you're it' in a game? Or does he mean 'it' like some kind of unknown beast?"

No one had time to answer me. The doors popped open, and we all ran through. I skidded to a halt inside.

The room was big and very dimly lit. There were large squares, circles, boxes, and columns to hide behind. There were tubes to crawl into and other shapes with holes cut in them. I was wrong. This game was going to be a blast!

Barry and I rolled out to our right and shot down that wall until we reached something that looked like a cave with an opening at each end.

"This will be perfect," Barry said. "If he sees us at one end, we can escape out the other side."

I agreed and we moved inside. I went first as far back as I could go until something grabbed me. I let out a small eek before I heard the voice.

"Hey, this is our spot," Frankie said.

"What do you mean 'our spot'?" I asked.

"The three of us got here first," she said. "But there is plenty of room for everyone."

Just then we heard a ghoulish cackle. "It" had just entered the room. We heard "it" grab one kid and then another. We could hear their screams echoing throughout the room. They sounded horrible. "It" was taking care of our friends one by one.

Soon everyone was caught but us. We could hear

"it" move throughout the room. We held our breaths and waited. I sank back deeper into one of the pockets inside the tunnel cave.

As I moved, I backed into someone. I figured it was one of the others. I whispered, "I'm sorry." In the dark it was hard to tell where people moved to.

Whoever was taking up the space behind me wasn't as polite as I was. He or she gave me a big push, and my body slammed into the others.

"What are you doing?" Davis said in a growling, stern whisper.

"It wasn't me. One of you pushed me. Whoever was behind me pushed me into you," I answered.

"That's impossible because we were all standing here whispering to each other," Lisa said with a degree of doubt in her voice.

"Then who pushed me?" I was afraid to ask, but I needed to know.

A cold, dead voice arose behind us. "I did," it croaked out.

"Run! It's a ghost!" I yelled to the others.

We went flying down the cave passageway. Frankie was in the lead. Each turn or twist in the passage was discovered when her body slammed hard against the fake stone wall.

The rest of us followed her lead, screaming and sucking in air as we tore from our hiding place. At one point, the wall of the cave came up too soon on Frankie, and she wasn't able to slow down or ram a softer part of her body into it. Even from the back I could hear her cries of pain as she hit the wall and fell back against Barry, who was right behind her. The two of them landed on the floor.

Both Davis and Lisa were able to avoid crashing down on top of them. I wish that I could have said the same for me.

My foot struck Frankie. I heard her whimper of pain just before I became airborne and flew across the top of them. The floor jumped up and met my face. I crunched against the concrete and groaned.

As I rolled on my back, I checked my nose to see if anything was broken inside it. I was okay, but I wanted to know about the others.

"Are you two all right?" I asked.

"We were until someone flew over the top of us," Davis quipped only seconds before we heard the ghost growling behind us. "We better get out of here," he finished.

The three of us raced down the rest of the passageway. Maybe knowing that the ghost was getting closer made us run so fast. In a few seconds we were right behind the other two and just a few yards from the mouth of the cave. We would be safe once we got out—I thought.

Just as Lisa exited the cave, I saw a silhouette move across the opening. She smacked into it and bounced off, crashing into Barry. Barry flew backward against Frankie, and she crashed into Davis, who in turn became the wall of flesh that I ran into.

In the next second, all five of us were lying on the cave floor, and the silhouette was standing above us. The "it" or the ghost had us for sure. I decided right then that if I lived to see thirteen, I wouldn't have any more birthday parties, especially at Spookie the Clown's Halls of Pizza.

I heard Lisa groan from the front of our tangled mess, "What or whom did I hit?"

"Hey, ho, hey, kids! It's just me, Spookie the

Clown. You guys won Hide and Shriek, excuse me, I mean Hide and Seek. Everyone else is caught and gone. Not even the 'it' is here," he told us.

"Then who was chasing us?" Davis asked.

"Only the six of us are in here," the clown answered.

I didn't believe him because I could hear the heavy, gasping, raspy breathing of the ghost behind us. Spookie's presence was keeping it from attacking us.

I started to push my way out from under the others. I stumbled back into the cave, and as I struggled to my feet, the ghost spoke to me, "Birthday boy, I'll be back. I'll bring you my gift later. I'll stop by for some birthday cake and I scream." Then I heard it move away and back into the cave.

"Let's get out of here, and I mean now," I commanded the others.

"That's right. It's time to play Musical Chairs," Spookie cheerfully reported.

"No, I mean out of this Halls of Pizza place," I snapped at him.

"I'm sorry, but I can't let you do that. There is still so much more of the party planned, and we wouldn't want to disappoint any of our guests. So, let's get up and go into our game room," Spookie said. Since none of us knew the way out, we had to follow him.

When we entered the game room, I hoped to see

the other guests waiting for us, but the room was empty. "Where are the others?" I asked.

"'It' got them," the bizarre clown said without any sign of worry or concern. I tried to press the question again, but Spookie put his hand over my mouth as he said, "Our last game will be Musical Chairs, but I have a special version. We set up five chairs. You all jump into one of them when the music stops. But one of the remaining chairs is—well, let's just say that you'll feel the earth move beneath your feet. Or rather beneath your seat."

"A trapdoor?" Frankie questioned in my direction. I shrugged to let her know that I didn't know what he meant.

"We also call this game Musical Chairs that dance," Spookie reported. "Now, take your places everyone. It is time to play."

Reluctantly, we circled the chairs when the music started. With each note our tension grew, for we knew that one of us was headed for trouble, but which one?

The music stopped. We all flew toward the chairs and sat. I looked around, and we were all still there. I guessed that the trapdoor system wasn't working. Unfortunately, I guessed wrong because in the next instant the other four chairs dropped through the floor, sending my friends to who knew where.

I gripped the sides of the seat, but my hands were

covered in sweat. They kept slipping off. The chair rocked a little. I gasped and prepared to jump off the chair when I looked up and saw Spookie and the clown team all around me.

Suddenly, the trapdoor seemed like the better of the two options. They got within a few feet of me when my chair went out from under me and I went flying down a slick and cold but very fast sliding board.

Flashing lights were along the side. They blinked quickly in unison.

I turned my attention to where I was heading. I shouldn't have.

About ten yards from my feet was a ball of flames with arms reaching out of the center of it. I was heading toward it, and I was not able to stop. I dug my heels into the slide, but it was too slick and I was going too fast.

I tried grabbing the side, but nothing was sticking out to hold on to. I was only a yard away. It had been a good twelve years, but in a few moments it would all come to an end.

I was inches away from the circle of fire.

20

I kept sliding and waiting to feel the scorching heat of the flames and the grasping hands of the monsters inside the flickering death I headed toward. I slid for another few seconds, then I felt the slide go out from under me as my body was hurled into the air. I was too afraid to open my eyes.

In the next instant I found myself bouncing onto something soft. Had my mind played tricks on me? My answer came quickly when a bunch of hands started gripping and pulling at me.

"No, leave me alone. I don't want to die!" I screamed, tugging desperately to escape the tightening grips.

"What are you talking about?" Frankie asked.

I opened my eyes, and my four friends were standing around me, trying to pull me up off the soft pillow that I landed on.

"What happened? Where are we? The last thing I remember was seeing a ball of fire with hands waiting to grab me. Where am I now?" I asked in a hurried and scared voice.

"We don't know. We just got here," Lisa said, pointing to orange strips around my pillow. "These can look a lot like flames if there's a fan blowing them."

Frankie added, "That ball of fire thing was really frightening. I can see why you were scared."

"Who was scared?" I asked in an attempt to cover it up.

"You were," Barry blurted out.

"You're right. I was petrified," I said as they pulled me to my feet. "Spookie the Clown's Halls of Pizza is not at all what I thought it was going to be like when I first heard of it. This place scares me to death. How in the world did those little kids from the party before us make it out of here without their hair standing on end?"

"They're braver than we are?" Lisa tossed out as a possibility.

Davis had been looking around the room and called back to us, "Hey, I don't know where we are, but I do know where we are heading. There is one door out of here, and it is marked the Halls of Fear. That sounds like a nice place to visit. I wonder if it is anywhere near the Tombs of Torture?"

"I'm scared of fear," Lisa added.

"Fear? They say that there is nothing to 'fear but fear itself,' Lisa, but here's one that's even better:

First John 4:18, 'Perfect love takes away fear.' Come on, let's try to find some other way out of here," Barry said. So Barry had been studying the Bible too.

"Don't you remember what we learned at youth group a few weeks ago?" Frankie asked.

"That Davis still sleeps with a teddy bear?" Barry joked.

Frankie shot one of those quit-goofing-around looks. "Here we are facing the perfect place to use our faith, guys. What was that Scripture again, Barry? We've all got to learn it."

"First John 4:18: 'Perfect love takes away fear.' Everyone got it?" Barry asked. He made sure we all nodded.

I tugged on the others and got us moving. "We better get going before Spookie and his clowns come for us."

Barry added, "Or worse, the two ghosts."

Frankie and I hurried along behind the others. I asked her, "You're not as afraid as I am. Is there anything that scares you all the way through?"

Frankie looked around as if she didn't want anyone else to hear her. "I do have this silly fear of the . . . you'll laugh if I tell," she said and then tried to get away without finishing it.

I shook my head no to make her believe I wouldn't laugh.

She continued. "I'm afraid of the dark. I keep imagining that there is someone at the top of our steps, and he is waiting for me."

My mouth dropped open. "I've got that same fear," I blurted out. Then I quietly told Frankie, "It's nice to be able to tell someone about it. I thought I was the only one in the world who still had that childhood fear left."

"Listen, if you two are finished playing secret pals, could we get the show on the road? One of us needs to enter the Hall of Fear and tell the others what it's like. I think it should be the birthday boy since it was his party that got us into all this," Barry insisted.

Barry pulled the door open, and all I could see was an extremely dark room with a little light coming in from our dark little landing strip.

Frankie was standing right behind me. She said, "I'll go in with you."

We went in a few steps, but nothing happened. We went farther, and the others filled in the floor behind us. Each of us looked around.

Lisa cried out, "Over there. I see something blinking. It's a tiny light!"

We moved in the direction of the light and found a booth much like the one in the game room.

"This is the only way out of here," Davis said.

Barry laughed and asked, "How do you know that?"

Davis pointed to something on the door of the booth that said, "This Is the Only Way Out."

Barry laughed again and said, "I guess you're right. Do we have any other choice?" Barry moved inside the booth.

Lisa stopped the rest of us from going in. "I don't think we should all go in at one time. Let's split up so that at least one of us survives Spookie's to tell the world what really goes on here."

Barry butted in, "Great idea, but it won't work. I've been looking at the control panel on this wall. The fuel gauge on this baby says empty, and by the looks of the controls, it must be preprogrammed. It may not land back here in this room. We have no choice but to risk all of us at once."

I let out a long breath of air and could hear the others doing the same thing. Everything in Spookie's place led to more fear. I wished that I had never booked my party here. I wished that I had never read chapter thirteen in that book. And I wished that we would all make it out of this place in one piece.

We went in, and the door slid shut behind us. Even though we expected it to shut on us, we jumped. I could tell that my friends and I had hit the point where our fears had taken over our imaginations.

The red numbers before us went from ten to nine to eight, then down to zero. We could feel the booth start to shake and rumble. Each of us shook from fright as much as from the booth.

The viewing screen opposite us showed that we had climbed slowly until we passed through the roof and were still climbing into the air. The buildings, cars, and people below us looked smaller and smaller. And without warning the booth stopped in midair.

"What happened?" I asked. I was so frightened that I could feel the same dizziness that I felt when I went looking for Davis behind Spookie's building.

"It looks like we are at the top of a pole," a high, shrill voice said. It took me a few seconds to recognize Davis as the speaker.

"How do you know?" I asked.

He was talking fast. It was almost like a scream. "Way over there, I can see some others in the same condition we are in," Davis answered me as he pointed across the skyline.

"Now what?" Barry cried with exasperation.

"We wait for this to go down, and when it does, we make a beeline out of here," I told the others. "And I mean out of here altogether."

"What about everyone else?" Frankie reminded me. I didn't want to hear the question. She was right. We had to get all of our friends out as well.

"Then let's get out of the Hall of Fears as fast as we can," I said as if I was nearly defeated.

"Here's an unusually dumb question, but why is this place called the Hall of Fears? I know I'm scared to death, but what kind of place is a Hall of Fears?" Lisa said as she choked back tears.

"The fear of heights is pretty bad for some people," Frankie told her. She tried to sound as calm as possible to soothe Lisa.

"But we are just sitting here and not doing anything. I want down before it starts to rock back and forth. Ahhh! I should never have said that. We're starting to rock," Lisa yelled.

"Calm down. A little wobble would be normal at this height," Davis said, trying to reassure her. The whole booth tipped so far to one side that we all screamed while we slid around and smashed into his body. The booth was going to break off the pole, and we were goners for sure.

21

We gripped each other, but it didn't stop the fear from gripping us too. The booth rocked to the other side, and we slid against that part of our future tomb. I did not like it, and I wanted out. Now!

"We've got to get out of here," I yelled while beads of perspiration ran down my forehead.

"How?" Barry screamed back. The terror poured out along with his question.

Davis was scrambling to get to a button on the control panel. It was flashing red.

"Davis, what are you trying to do?" I yelled.

"This might be the way down. We've got to try it." His finger almost reached it when we dipped backward and we all slid along the wall until our heads touched the top of the booth. When it tipped forward, Davis could easily push the button since he landed on top of it.

We felt the booth straighten back up and then start to descend. We cheered, but our joy didn't last long.

We were dropping at such a rapid rate that our land ing could flatten us permanently.

"What else can happen? It can't get worse," Frankie called out.

"Yes, it can," Lisa yelled back.

She was shaking like a flag in the wind. She shrieked, "Our little booth is starting to break up. Look! It's cracking up!"

I looked between my feet to where Lisa pointed and saw cracks developing. One moved from where we sat to the other side of the booth. Then another went from side to side. The cracks on the walls looked like lightning bolts flashing through the sky. They went every way imaginable and just as quickly.

We didn't have much time left, and we were too high in the air to make it to the ground before the booth split apart.

"Got to hang on to something!" Davis bellowed.

I looked around, but the only thing that I really wanted to hang on to was my life. Down farther and farther, faster and faster. The booth could not take the pressure of our rapid fall, and it cracked open.

The sudden splitting of the booth startled me. I could see the sky all around us, and then the seat we were on fell away from us. There was nothing to grip. Nothing to hold. Nothing but a disastrous end to a dismal drop.

I closed my eyes and waited for the impact. The impact that would cut my life short at age twelve.

I hit the ground much sooner than I expected. I quickly moved my hands to my arms and legs to see if I was intact. Then I reached for my head. It was still on. I finally felt brave enough to open my eyes.

I couldn't believe it. I sat up and saw that the other four were right beside me, all in perfect shape. The whole time the booth was only a few feet off the ground, and it was all done with special effects.

"What was that all about?" Barry asked.

"Fear," answered Frankie. "We are in the Hall of Fears. We faced the fear of heights, the fear of falling, and the fear of death. What's left?"

As he was walking toward an opening that hadn't been there earlier, Davis said, "I don't care what is next as long as it leads us out of here."

I wished that he was predicting our future. The rest of us were already scrambling behind him when we passed through the new passageway into an extremely dark room. We could hear the wind whistling and the flapping of bat wings all around us.

"Where did we end up this time?" I asked.

No one answered. We all heard the sound of steps accompanied by heavy, deep breathing. It had to be one of the ghosts. The sound got closer and closer. The ghost that inhabited the darkness of the room headed our way.

I tapped someone on the shoulder. I shouldn't have. I felt the person's body stiffen and jerk away from me while yelling, "Ahhh!" It was Lisa.

"I'm sorry," I apologized. "I just wanted to know what was happening." The others answered with three different guesses.

"We're lost in the dark," Frankie snapped.

I didn't need to see her to know that she was on edge. Her fear of the dark was tensing her voice, making it sound high and strained.

"There are ghosts and bats all around us, and I hate both," sighed Davis. He seemed ready to give up.

Barry broke in, "I don't care what's going on. I simply want to find the way out, and that I'm going to do."

Anything else that Barry wanted to say had to wait. An excruciating screech cut through the darkness. "Run!" somebody yelled, but it wasn't necessary. We were already slapping our tennis shoe soles on the hard ground beneath us.

None of us knew where we were headed, but we

knew what we were running from. It was dangerous to race through the darkness, but the peril that sounded so close made us throw away our caution.

I could hear someone just ahead of me. She was encouraging herself by saying, "Run, Frankie, run," aloud. I made a quick decision and followed Frankie's voice.

A thought flashed in my mind. My birthday party was more like a nightmare than a party. I wished that Spookie's had turned out to be some place safe and nice. Maybe a little pizza and a little birthday cake and Pin the Tail on the Donkey would have been fun. Having ghostly figures chasing us was not fun. It was terrifying.

"Frankie, wait up. I don't hear anything behind us any longer."

I heard her feet come to a stop, and I skidded as near to them as possible. "Where are you?" I asked her.

"MacKenzie, I don't know. It's so dark in here. Very dark and I'm petrified," she said, sobbing.

I wanted to tell her how much I agreed when a bloodcurdling scream crackled through the darkness.

"Help," came a scream from Barry. "I've been caught."

"What do we do?" Frankie asked.

"We've got to find him. If we move to one side or

the other, we'll find a wall. Maybe we can find a door or a light switch," I answered.

We slid along the wall using our hands as if they were eyes. I hoped to find a door. I was praying that we would discover the way out.

"Help," I heard the scream again. Then I felt something on my shoulder. I spun around, expecting to hear Frankie's voice.

"Birthday boy, have you found the treasure yet?"

I gulped as the hands of the ghost gripped my shoulders and squeezed them together.

It had to be one of the ghosts. I shook off the hands, turned back around, and saw a ghostly figure staring at me. It was glowing in the dark.

My blood ran cold. My body stiffened. Now the ghoul had Frankie in his grasp. I panicked.

"Let her go!" I demanded as I lunged forward, trying to grab. The only thing in my mind was that I had to save my friend. I missed the ghost and crashed to the floor.

I whipped my head up to see where Frankie was. The ghost was dragging her, kicking and screaming, with him. "Wait, I'm the birthday boy. Take me, not her."

His sinister laugh cut into me. "Birthday boy, come and take her away."

In the next second the darkness engulfed them, and the ghost disappeared. I ran to where he was standing. I didn't stop in time. I smashed into another wall.

The pain shot through my aching body and rattled me so hard that I thought my teeth would eject like jet pilots from their airplanes. I shook my head to get my senses back. I was feeling the wall for a button in hope of finding where he went.

"I don't think that this is part of the birthday party games." The voice startled me, and I nearly had a cardiac arrest.

"Barry, is that you?" I blurted out. Not waiting for him to answer, I asked, "Where are the others?"

"Right here. We saw the ghoul drag Frankie in this direction and ran toward it," Davis answered.

"We've got to find her," Lisa pleaded.

"We will. There has to be a door on this wall. He disappeared too fast. Help me find it," I urged.

My hands were running along the wall when they hit a button. I pushed it. The wall spun around, and I found myself standing on the other side. I sucked in a breath, then remembered why I was there. I had to find Frankie.

Suddenly, the room lightened slightly. I looked all over to see where it came from. I didn't see the ghost until he called me.

"Birthday boy."

The voice wasn't close, but I had to move toward it. I had a friend in trouble, and we had to stick together. My eyes started to adjust to the dim light. Before me was an entrance with a hallway. I couldn't believe it. I was standing on the other side of a maze. How could I find my way through it in near darkness?

"Perfect love takes away fear. Perfect love takes away fear," I heard myself repeating. It hit me. I had been in the midst of darkness for the last several minutes. I hadn't been in total panic because I had friends all around me. But now, it was dark, and I was alone facing the ghost. My sense of fear and dread began to swell inside. "Perfect love takes away fear!" I said firmly. The ruler of darkness wasn't going to rule me anymore!

I had to overcome the fear in order to save Frankie. My breath was coming in short gasps. I had never been so scared before.

"Help, Ralph!" I heard Frankie yell. Ralph? Who was Ralph? Then I got it. She could see me, but I couldn't see her. She could see the way through the maze. Ralph was an expression we used to call out directions. If you wanted someone to turn right, you said, "Hang a Ralph." Frankie was going to direct me through.

I went to my right, and it took me around several bends until I came to another choice. I needed help again.

I yelled, "Ralph, are you out there?" No sounds came back.

"Louie?" I called. Louie was the coded direction for

turning left. After I said Louie, I heard a muffled noise. I turned left.

That time I did not get far until I had to make another choice. "Louie," I yelled. No answer.

Then I called out, "Ralph." Still no answer. The ghost must have figured out our code.

I needed to make my own decision. I went to the right. I took five steps and came to a dead end. It was the wrong choice, but I had lost only a few seconds. I turned and ran back the other way.

My next choice came too quickly, but somehow Frankie got word to me. I heard her yell, "Ralph," and I moved that direction. I was getting closer. Her voice sounded near.

Winding my way through the maze, I came to what was obviously the end. The ghost knew I was there. He knew I was close. What would he try next?

I slipped out of the maze, and right in front of me was a dark staircase. At the top of the stairs I saw the glowing, ghastly figure with Frankie next to him.

24

"Birthday boy," the ghost called in his raspy, gasping voice. "I'm waiting for you to come to me. I want to exchange your friend for the treasure. Come on, birthday boy."

"We don't have any treasure. We didn't come for any treasure," I pleaded.

He only cackled and pushed Frankie in front of him so I could see her at the top of the nearly dark staircase. "Here she is."

"Let her go!" I screamed, trying to make myself sound menacing.

He howled in earsplitting laughter.

The ghost was taunting me, but I was too afraid to go up the steps. All my life, I'd had that terrible nightmare of a monster at the top of a dark stairway. I never thought that I would have to face it.

The fear was overwhelming. My heart beat like a big bass drum, but I had to do it. If I did not climb the steps, the ghost could harm Frankie.

To save her, I had to walk up a dark stairway. I

could never make that trek up the steps in my dreams. Could I do it in real life?

I took the first step. My legs went weak. My knees seemed to turn into jelly. I had to take another step and another one.

My breath was coming in fast bursts, and that was making my head spin. I wasn't sure that I could make it without fainting. I prayed as I made two more steps.

The figure loomed even larger as I got closer. My shaking was getting worse. But I had to beat my fear. I had to face the figure at the top of the stairs.

"Birthday boy, is it time for you to give back my treasure? Are you bringing it to me?" the ghost taunted.

I wanted to fire back a witty and tough retort like a hero in a spy movie, but I was at a loss for words. The words would have gotten stuck in my dry mouth and swelling throat anyway.

I closed my eyes, lowered my head, and charged up the remaining steps. I planned to ram myself into the ghost. Then again, if it was a ghost, I would pass right through it. So I snapped my eyes open to see if the door at the top of the stairs would hurt when I hit it.

The ghost wasn't there. When I reached the top, I turned to see what happened. Frankie was standing there next to me, and a set of really dark stairs was below me—but no ghost.

"Frankie, where did the ghost go?" I asked frantically.

"He went through that door, MacKenzie. And by the way, thanks," Frankie told me. Neither one of us had a moment to think about what had just happened. We needed to go through the door.

"We've got to get out of here. Our best bet is to go through that door just like the ghost did," I told Frankie.

"Where are the others?" she asked.

"I don't know. They were right behind me when I entered the room, and then they were gone. I think the door slammed on them, and they couldn't find the way into the maze. We'll find them later," I responded. Although my mind was worried about the other three, I knew that we needed to get free in order to help them.

"Let's go, MacKenzie. I'll be glad to follow you through that door, and I do mean follow," Frankie attempted to lighten the moment.

We both needed to have our tension reduced. A good laugh always helped except that, right then, I didn't feel like laughing.

"Here goes nothing," I said. My hand pressed on the door, and it popped open.

"Careful. The ghost may be waiting for you on the other side," she reminded me.

I eased it open inch by inch while holding my

breath. I was ready to push it all the way open when I closed my eyes.

Frankie tapped me on the shoulder and said, "Keep your eyes open. We need you to be wide-eyed for this."

She was right. I opened my eyes and pushed the door the rest of the way open. It was another dimly lit room, but I could see nothing inside. I grabbed Frankie, and we entered the room.

I took a few steps farther in when a hand reached out from behind the door and grabbed me.

25

The hand spun my body around and I was staring at him. He said, "Ho, hey, ho! We thought we lost you for a little while. It's time to open your present from Spookie."

The lights came up in the room. I could see that we were back in the Hall of Food.

"Where is everyone?" I asked with my voice showing my anger.

"Don't worry about them. They're tied up in another room. We want you to open your gift. It's from everyone here at Spookie the Clown's Halls of Pizza. We want you to know how much we appreciated being able to give you this very special party. It isn't every day that a group of your fame is in here," he said.

What he said confused me. What kind of special group were we? I was a kid having his twelfth birthday party like millions of other kids. And what did he mean about our friends being tied up?

115

I was ready to ask him what he meant, but a large box shoved into my hands distracted me. "What's this?" I asked.

"That's the gift I was just telling you about. Come on in here and sit down in your chair," Spookie said. He directed me back to the big chair that I had been in earlier.

I sat down in the seat with the big box on my lap.

Frankie dropped next to me and put her mouth next to my ear. "Just play along. We need to buy some time until we can figure a way out of this room and then get our friends free."

"Go ahead and open it," Spookie encouraged.

I was afraid to do it. It could have been a box of snakes, exploding bombs, insects, or anything. I just stared at it.

"Hey, are you going to open it?" Frankie asked.

"Would you?" I responded.

"No, but then again, I'm not the birthday boy, am I?" she said.

I looked up at Spookie the Clown and said, "I want to know where all my friends and guests are. It will be very difficult to explain their disappearance to all those parents."

"Disappearance? No one disappeared," he said. "Now go ahead and open the gift."

Right, no one disappeared. Did he think that I was born yesterday?

"What about the ghost that almost grabbed us in the cave during Hide and Seek and then did grab Frankie just before we came in here?" I asked.

I was surprised at myself. Going up those stairs in the dark and trusting the Lord to protect me had really changed something inside me. I felt as if I was filled with new inner strength and courage.

"Okay, if you aren't going to open the gift, we'll have more cake and ice cream. Bring in the food," he yelled.

The clown waiters and waitresses rolled two big carts into the room. One had a cake on it in the shape of Spookie's head. The other cart held a gigantic tub of vanilla ice cream.

"Okay, birthday boy, you cut the cake and give yourself and your guest a piece, and then you get to dish out the ice cream. That's a tradition here at Spookie's," he said.

"You've only been open a week. How could you have traditions already?" Frankie asked.

"We are very old in our hearts. Now the cake," he insisted.

I expected something to jump out of it when I sank the knife into the thick white icing and then through the chocolate cake. I sliced off two pieces for Frankie and me and dropped them on the plates.

"Now for the ice cream," Spookie said as he slapped the ice-cream scoop into my hand. "Dig in, but I want to warn you that the ice cream is very hard, so thrust that scoop in it with all your might."

Shaking my head yes, I thought Spookie was a very strange clown. I've dug out ice cream before. Why was he making a federal case out of how to scoop ice cream? I started thinking that Spookie should have been Loony the Clown.

"Listen, Spookie, I think I can dig ice cream out without any instruction booklet or training course," I snapped toward him. Then I stepped up to the ice-cream vat. It was a large circle of vanilla ice cream. It wasn't that high, and the cart that it was on wasn't very tall.

I leaned over the ice cream and asked Frankie, "How much do you want?"

"I like ice cream, so give me two or three scoops," she responded.

I looked at Spookie next and said, "You are welcome to some cake and ice cream. Of course, at the Halls of Pizza it would be better to call it birthday cake and I scream."

"No, thanks. Just go ahead and serve yourselves," he said through his clown makeup smile.

"Here goes nothing," I said as I brought the scoop down hard on the frozen ice cream. The scoop sank into the ice cream as if it was nothing but a milk-shake. Then my hand sank, and finally, I was dipped up to my elbow in the white foam.

I thought it was another of Spookie's stupid jokes. I was pulling my hand out of the ooze when I felt something grip my arm deep inside the ice cream. I pulled myself back until I could see the long sharp, nails of the ghost showing above the surface of the ice cream.

I wrestled and pulled, trying to free my arm, but in the next instant my arm was sinking back into the vat. Deeper and deeper I kept going until I felt the gooey ooze at my ear.

"I told you that I was coming back. And guess what? Here I am," the ghost's raspy voice gurgled in the white foaming goo. "I want some birthday boy in my ice cream."

The next thing I knew, two hands had gripped my shoulders and pulled me from the fake ice cream. The ghost tugged one more time, but his hand slipped from my arm and my arm popped out of the ooze. I stumbled backward and dropped to the floor.

Spookie was wiping me off and apologizing as his helpers wheeled the cart of ice cream out of the room. "I'm sorry," he said. "Our ice cream always comes frozen solid. I thought it would be the same. Someone must have left it out, and it thawed. I'm so sorry about that."

"Didn't you see the hand come out of the vat and grab me?" I asked frantically.

"About the only thing that could have been in

there was a wild vanilla bean, but I don't believe they are strong or vicious enough to pull someone in. Your forceful thrust of the hand made you lose your balance, and you fell in," he explained apologetically. "Besides, those tubs of ice cream are so shallow that nothing could have been inside it."

"Shallow? I was being pulled in by some kind of strange ghost. It was the same thing that grabbed Frankie in the Hall of Fear and pushed me while we were playing Hide and Seek."

"What you're saying is impossible. I'll show you. BooBoo the Clown, bring that vat of ice cream back in here."

BooBoo answered, "Sorry, great clown boss, but we already tossed that stuff in the garbage can out back."

"I guess I can't prove anything to you, but we can get this wild and crazy party going again. Let's get back to the gift. Go ahead and open it." Spookie was all smiles.

"After the ice-cream thing, I'm not sure that I want to open the gift." I balked at doing what he asked.

"Go ahead. Open it. I picked it out especially for you. Here, I'll help." Spookie grabbed the gift from my lap and started opening it.

I grabbed it back.

"Okay, I'll open it," I snapped at him. I pulled the ribbon off and tossed it to the floor.

Then I started ripping at the paper. It fell away quickly until the box top was the next item to be removed.

Gulping in a large breath of air, I pulled the top off the box, revealing a Spookie the Clown plastic snow globe.

In the next instant there was a roar of noise all around me.

26

I jumped three feet out of the chair, and then my shoes hit the floor. I whipped my body around to see what was making all the noise. All the guests at my party had entered from another room.

"MacKenzie, this is the greatest party I've ever been to," several of them said in unison.

Barry and Davis ran up to me. "Mac, watch out. It all looks like just a fun time but don't forget the ghost," Davis whispered.

All the others were finding their seats. They were very noisy, but I could tell that they were having a great time. Barry plopped down next to me.

"What happened to you guys? I thought we were staying together. I walked into that maze alone in the dark." My voice was a mixture of anger and frustration

He smiled at me and said, "I'm really sorry, but right after you walked in, the door slammed shut. We tried to get it to open, but nothing worked. Spookie grabbed us and said that you would be waiting for us. Then we all went back to the Hall of Games for a while."

"What happened to all the others? Where were they?" I asked.

"Much the same but I can tell you for sure that they had a blast. Most of them keep saying that they want their next birthday here too. I think you've started a real fad," Barry informed me.

"Do you mean it was all just a joke or something?" I asked.

"No, it wasn't a joke," Davis added. "None of them had the experiences with the ghost, and none of them went through the Hall of Fear. To them it was the most fantastic birthday celebration they ever went to. You're going to be a legend. The whole school is going to know about the kind of parties that you throw."

"Personally, I just want out of here. Before you came in, the ghost pulled me into a vat of melted ice cream. Spookie acted as if he didn't see the long fingernailed hand grab me," I whispered until Spookie called for our attention.

"I hate to say that our party is almost over. If you enjoyed yourself, tell others. If you didn't like the place, don't tell anyone," Spookie said as he broke into his goofy laugh. "Ho, hey, ho!"

"I don't hate to say that this party is over," Frankie

whispered to the rest of us. "Spookie acts as if he doesn't even know what is going on. He seems oblivious to the ghost roaming around in his Halls of Pizza."

Spookie said, "But before we all have to head back to our houses, I want to do one last magic trick. I need a volunteer. Well, not actually a volunteer because someone made a special request for MacKenzie Griffin to be a part of this trick."

"What do I do?" I asked the other four.

"I don't think Spooky knows about the ghost, so he can't be in on it. This trick ought to be pretty safe. Go ahead and finish out the party with one last blast," Barry advised.

"If the ghost eats me, our friendship is over. You won't be my best friend anymore," I warned Barry.

He responded, "If the ghost eats you, can I have your new bike?"

I didn't have a chance to answer. The clown helpers surrounded me and lifted my chair into the air. They carried me across the room and sat me on a platform next to Spookie.

He waved his hand in my direction and said, "This is a very simple trick. I will lay this piece of cloth over MacKenzie "

He dropped a thick, black piece of material over me. As it hit my head, I felt the platform start to lower, and Spookie's voice trailed off. I looked up, and a wire shaped like the back of the chair gave the illusion that I was still sitting in position.

The platform lowered into a dingy little room below the floor. I could see a tall, dark shape in the poorly lit corner.

I had a bad feeling. I knew that I had seen the silhouette before, and it was the last human being, or at least former human being, that I wanted to see.

He was lowering me by pushing a red button. Once I struck bottom, he turned to look at me, took a large step closer, and said, "Where is my treasure?"

"I don't have your treasure. We never found any treasure," I screamed at the ghost. "I don't know why you think we have it, but I would like to just get out of here."

"I can't let that happen."

"Any second now, Spookie is going to bring this platform back to the floor, and I better be in the chair or . . . or . . . or . . ."

"Or what?" the ghost snapped quickly in an icy voice. "I control the platform with this button." The ghost pointed a long, sharp nail at the green button. "Where is my treasure?"

"What treasure? I don't have any treasure," I pleaded.

My eyes were filling with tears. But I couldn't cry. I couldn't let him know how frightened I was.

The ghoul stared deep into my eyes. He opened his mouth and sneered out, "I want the treasure that Penny the Party Crasher gave you."

He wanted the tokens. All he wanted was the tokens. I dug into my left pocket. None there. I must have put them in my right pocket. Not there. I thrust my hands deeply into every pocket in my clothing. Nothing.

I needed to think of another way out.

The ghost took another step closer, and I slid my chilling spine up the red velvet of the large backed chair until I was standing on the springy cushion.

When I stood, the plastic snow globe with Spookie and all his friends in it fell to the chair seat. Maybe the ghost would take that and leave me alone.

He didn't take the cheap globe. Instead, he started moving around me, dragging a sharp nail across my arm covered with goose bumps.

I kept one eye on the ghost and another on the green button. I moved toward the switch, and the ghost yanked me hard against the back of the chair.

"Don't think that you are going to get away until I have what I want," he said with that gritty, raspy, dead voice.

Think, MacKenzie! You've got to push that button, I said to myself. I tried to think, but the ghost's movements kept me from coming up with a solution. If only I could get to the green button.

I stretched my arm out, and the ghost gave my hand a crack.

"Naughty birthday boy, are you trying to leave so

soon? And just when I was enjoying myself. You are not a very good party host. You haven't offered me anything to eat," the gray, grim form teased.

As much as I hated soccer practice, even that sounded better than being at the mercy of this ghoul.

Soccer! That was it! That was my answer.

All I needed to do was kick the plastic Spookie orb across the little room and strike the green button with it. And I had to do it fast.

The ghost moved around to my left side, and I pretended to make a move to my right. He needed to leap behind the chair to stop me or at least stop what he thought I was doing. When he did that, I had a clear shot at the green button.

I kicked. Thwump!

The globe sailed through the air. I held my breath as the ghost saw the plastic ball leave my foot.

He knew that he had to stop it. He dived through the air. I watched it all as if it was an instant replay on TV.

The plastic ball was moving more slowly than the ghost, and his flying body was catching up. The distance between them shrank another inch and then another inch. But the distance to the button grew shorter at the same time.

I held my breath, and I closed my eyes. I didn't want to see what would happen. It was my only chance to escape the ghost. If it failed, I had no other chances to succeed.

Then I heard the plastic ball hit. Did it hit the button? Or did it hit the wall? Did the ghost knock it to the ground?

All I could do was pray.

I felt the platform and chair jerk. I started to move upward.

The ghost was lying on the floor. He tried to regain his footing, but the plastic orb had smashed, splashing the liquid from inside all over the floor. He slipped on it and fell.

Ascending into the black cloth, I could hear Spookie say, "I think our birthday boy has finally returned from the great beyond. I've never had anyone take so long to disappear and come back before. I do hope . . ."

Spookie the Clown did not even finish his statement before I ripped the black cloth off me and started running for the exit.

"Where are you going, MacKenzie?" Spookie asked.

"This is the time my mother said that she would be here. She hates it when I'm late. In fact, she grounds me. So I better leave right now," I yelled over my shoulder as I ran out.

When I got to the door, I stopped and motioned for everyone to follow. The entire group of party guests raced out behind me.

I smashed open the door and bolted through it. I didn't get very far. On the other side of the door I smacked into something. The impact sent me backward.

I was stumbling to hold my balance when someone came through the door behind me. His body met mine, and I bounced forward falling facedown with my forehead lying on a toe. One of the ghosts was waiting for me in the foyer.

All the kids who entered the foyer behind me let out a muffled scream when they saw me sprawled at the feet of the legendary, not-so-mythical creature.

We were all doomed. I had conquered my fear of the dark and the ghost at the top of the stairs only to be wiped out by a ghost inches from the exit.

I started to push myself up from the floor in an attempt to escape. Then I heard someone say, "So, how was the party, kiddo?"

Only one person ever called me kiddo. It was my mom. I scrambled to my feet. The only thing that I wanted to do was to get out of Spookie's.

I didn't have to tell my mother anything about the party. All the other kids were telling their parents about the fantastic time they had. Most of them asked to have their next party at Spookie's.

I smiled and nodded my head. My party was a

hit. I might have been scared to death by one of the ghosts haunting the building, but everyone else had a great time.

"We better get going, but first I need to pay and thank Spookie for the great time that all of you had," my mom said.

Frankie and Lisa walked up behind me. Lisa asked, "Did you have another run-in with the ghost while you were under that cloth?"

"Yes, I thought I was a goner for sure."

"So did we," Barry said as Davis put his hand on my shoulder.

"Listen, I'll get Mom away from the ghouls, and we all can go home," I told them as I walked to the pass-through window where Mom was paying for the party.

Spookie had handed her a business card, and she slid it to me to carry home. As my mom was writing a check, I read the desk calendar by the phone. I wondered what other groups would have to face the ghosts of Spookie's Halls of Pizza.

Suddenly, my mouth dropped open, and my head became light. I couldn't believe what I was reading. Written over today's date was "National Horror Movie Fan Club Birthday Party." Underneath was a memo that said, "Rent ghost costumes and really scare the kids." Across Saturday's date was written my name.

Spookie had written the wrong party groups on the wrong days. I got the party for the Horror Movie Fan Club.

The greatest birthday party of my life was all a mistake. Cool!

I smiled at her and said, "Mom, we're ready to go."

"Good, wait for me in the van. I'll only be a few seconds," she responded in her usual joyful way.

As I walked up to the others, I looked down at Spookie's business card. Below the words *Spookie the Clown's Halls of Pizza* was imprinted *Alexander S. Pookie, Owner and Chief Executive Clown*. I chuckled to myself. The Spookie name had nothing to do with ghosts. It was actually the clown's name, S. Pookie.

I told the others, "Mom said for us to wait for her in the van."

We all started to exit, but before I left, I wanted to look around at the greatest party place in the world. Just then something light floated down on my head.

Looking up at the stuffed heads on the walls, I expected to see Spookie in the one over the double doors to the Hall of Food. I gasped.

For a second I thought I saw one of the gray clown ghosts with its head through the hole, and it winked at me. I blinked and looked back. Nothing was there.

I shook my head and noticed that a flower petal flipped off the top of it and floated down before my

133

face. Maybe the ghost is really a . . . no, forget about it. I won't even allow myself to think about it.

I whistled and strolled out the doors to the sidewalk. As the doors swung shut behind me, I was sure I heard someone say in a raspy, gritty, dead voice, "Birthday boy." I ran to the van.

When he began to swing back toward the ground Clint let go of the vine. He landed inside the jail tree's ring of vines. Say, this made a pretty good hiding place. If the swamp weren't so spooky, he wouldn't mind a hideaway like this.

"Man," Hammer puffed. He moved slowly toward Clint. "I thought you were done for. I thought one of the snake ghosts had taken control of the vine."

Hammer shuffled closer to Clint. He held out a hand. "Hey, Clint? You okay? You didn't break any bones, did you?"

"Nah," Clint croaked. He clasped Hammer's hand and hauled himself to his feet. He looked at his hands. They were covered with green plant stains. It was nothing but a vine after all.

Clint went back to the vine and gave it a push. It swayed gently. He forced strength into his voice. "A vine."

"What?" Hammer didn't catch what Clint said.

"Never mind. Check this place out, Hammer. It's kind of neat. You can almost hide in here."

Hammer looked around the dark enclosure of vines.

"I see what you mean. But I don't think it's neat. I think it's creepy. Come on, let's get to the cabin and get this over with."

"Hold it, Hammer! Look!"

"Yikes!" said Hammer when he saw Clint's discovery. The soft, mossy mound within the vines was only camouflage. Clint had found the snake ghosts' tunnel.

"Come on, let's go," Clint said, putting his hand to the entrance to the tunnel.

"What? Are you out of your mind? You can't go in there! And you certainly can't open the door. Do you want the snake ghosts to know we've discovered their passageway?"

What Hammer said made sense. He wasn't convinced they were dealing with ghosts yet, but he still could've caused some serious trouble by disturbing the tunnel. Whoever or whatever used this tunnel was best kept in the dark about their having found it.

"Where do you suppose it leads?" Clint wondered.

"My theory is that it leads all over town. Of course, it depends how far the ghosts have gone in their conquests."

"Maybe you're right, Hammer. But since when

do ghosts need tunnels to move around? They can go through hard surfaces and be invisible if they want," Clint observed.

"That may be true," Hammer said, "but don't forget ghosts have their early stages when they're still transforming. Plus, they need a place where they can drag their . . . victims."

They both shuddered. Suddenly the hideaway didn't seem so cozy after all.

"Come on, we've found what you were looking for, haven't we? Let's go," Hammer said.

"Not yet. This just raises more questions. The cabin is only a short way from here. Let's go." Clint rejoined his friend.

They walked through more clumps of weeds and grass.

"Cut around to the right," Clint said.

He hadn't meant to speak so softly . . . as if he were afraid something would hear him.

Clint and Hammer crept around the jail tree. Clint thought they'd never get to the other side. Was the jail tree spreading too? Just like the whole swamp seemed to be?

At last they made it to the top of the little hill. They peered down at the cabin.

The roof looked much steeper than Clint remembered. It seemed to point toward the sky. It made the cabin look like a ghostly rocket.

"Three Bears' house, huh?" Hammer's voice made Clint jump. "They must have painted it with coal tar."

"Let's go." Clint started down the hill before he could lose his nerve. Hammer stayed at his side.

"Here's the first window I looked in," Clint said. "Kristin claims she saw three bears sitting on chairs in here."

"What?" Hammer said. "You're kidding, right?"

They cupped their hands around their eyes and pressed their faces to the window. As before, Clint felt dust creep up his nose and settle in his throat. He stepped back from the window and sneezed.

That same instant Hammer let out a scream.

SPINECHILLERS™

Levelheaded Clint Gleeson laughs at his excitable friend Hammer's assertion that the land his dad wants to buy is a swamp that's haunted and inhabited by the ghosts of snakes. But a crawling fear cuts short his laughter when he sees what couldn't possibly be so.

It's too late to worry about what *may* be out there in . . .

Stay Away from the Swamp

SpineChillers™ #8
by Fred E. Katz